# RETURN TO THE BEWILDERNESS

## A SHORT STORY ANTHOLOGY

## JOHN W. OTTE

GEEKY GRACE BOOKS

Print Edition: 979-8-9858103-7-0

Ebook Edition: 979-8-9858103-8-7

Book Cover by Muhammad Waqas

First edition 2026

For Joe and Lois

# CONTENTS

# FOREWORD

Welcome back to the Bewilderness!

If you're not familiar with the concept, allow me to explain. Back in 2018, I released a short story anthology entitled *Into the Bewilderness*. It comprised all the stories I had written and/or published over the previous few years. I released a second edition in 2023 with a snazzy new cover and notes explaining where the stories had come from. What inspired me? What challenges did I face? What was I thinking?

It's been almost eight years since I released our first trek into the Bewilderness. While I've mostly been focusing on writing novels, I still write short stories, especially as part of the NYC Midnight Short Story Challenge. Each time I've written one, I added it to a growing manuscript, promising that once I reached critical mass, I would release them into the wild.

That day has come. In your hands is a book that covers a wide variety of genres, visiting so many worlds, both familiar and bizarre. Notes follow each story about what inspired each tale and so on.

I hope you enjoy your return to the Bewilderness! Travel safe!

# Upstart

The world always tries to end when I got better things to do.

While I was heading home for lunch with my daughter, my handler called me. I groaned. Clarissa hadn't been home since Christmas! Sure, she'd be there all week for spring break, but still. Duty called, though, and I didn't have much choice.

I tapped the comm unit in my ear. "I'm here, Abadi. What's the situation?"

His precise voice was barely audible over the roar of the passing wind. "We've got actionable intelligence on the Baron."

No. I almost came to a halt, hovering over our neighborhood. The Baron! A malevolent genius who had used his scientific acumen to give himself incredible strength and nearly indestructible organic armor. He had been on the run for years, and his body count kept growing. He hadn't cracked five digits yet, but it wasn't from lack of trying. Hell, last time he came through town, he killed 247 people.

Including my Marjorie.

I shook my head to clear it. "When and where?"

"You know that big eclipse festival down at the Riverfront?"

My stomach flipped. Buncha hippy-dippies figured the eclipse was the harbinger of some spiritual awakening. Stupid as all get-out, but there'd be a sizeable crowd. Big target.

"The BND nabbed an arms dealer named Klaus von Hayek in Bonn yesterday. Von Hayek says the Baron purchased a doomsday weapon and plans to use it at the festival."

Okay, so find and defuse the bomb, capture the Baron. Do-able. But that left one factor in play: "What about the kid?"

There was a long pause, then Abadi spoke quietly. "No sign of Tsuki for the past few days, but—"

But we both knew that there was a leak in the agency. Someone kept feeding that newcomer intel, and he kept trying to outdo me. It wasn't that big a deal when Tsuki went after muggers and shoplifters. But the Baron was mine. No way was I going to let some unpowered brat show me up. Not today. Not with him.

I took off again, darting through a flock of geese. My back groaned in protest as I twisted in midair. Fifty-five had hit me like that comet hit the dinosaurs. Flying should have been easy thanks to my powers, but it definitely took a larger toll on my body.

"Patch me through to Clarissa, will you?"

Abadi grunted, but he did as I asked.

She didn't pick up, her phone going straight to voicemail. I smiled and said, "Sweetie, something's come up at the office. I'll be late for lunch. Keep it warm for me, okay?"

That would have to do. Being Mike Olson, empty nester who missed his daughter, would keep. By the might of Sol Invictus, I, Solarian, would bring the Baron to justice.

I arrived within minutes. Riverfront Park was crowded. Hundreds, if not thousands, of people milled about, chatting and laughing, unaware that death lurked in their midst. A few of them even pointed up at me as I flew overhead, waving and shouting my name. But I didn't acknowledge them. I couldn't.

"Sitrep?" Abadi's voice hissed in my ear.

"No sign up top. Any new intel?"

"Not much. The BND's pretty sure the device is big. This isn't a suitcase nuke. It'll probably be in a van."

I snarled. That narrowed it down. There were dozens of vehicles scattered throughout the park: food trucks, news vans, not to mention the hundreds of cars and vehicles in the parking lots.

A loud crack sounded behind me, and I swallowed a groan. Sure enough, someone wearing a full suit of high-tech armor sailed up next to me. I didn't even glance in his direction. I knew the details: dark blues and blacks, a crescent moon on his chest plate. A genuine hero wouldn't need gadgets to fight crime. But Tsuki was part of that new breed. They'd been pushing out too many of us with their flash and gimmicks. Not real heroes. Not to me.

Especially not him.

"Here to take in the festival?" I asked.

"We both know he's down there." Tsuki's voice warbled, distorted by some gizmo in his helmet.

I spun to face the upstart. I think he looked back. Damn featureless mask. I had no way of telling which way his eyes were pointing.

"Now see here, junior. I been hunting the Baron for a long time. He's mine."

"Then you'd better find him first."

With that, Tsuki jetted off, heading for the parking lots. Probably thought the bomb was in one of the SUVs.

But that didn't track. The Baron would want to maximize the death toll, so he wouldn't blow up a bunch of cars. He'd want the bomb in the middle of the crowd. I smirked. Let Tsuki waste his time checking parked cars. The wind tugged at me as I shot to my left, heading for the center of Riverfront. There! A cluster of four food trucks, three of which were surrounded by people. The fourth, a falafel truck, appeared closed in spite of the crowds around it. Either bad business or a disguise. That had to be it.

I dropped from the sky, landing a dozen yards from the target. Some passers-by shouted in surprise, but soon they murmured my name.

"Is that really Solarian?"

"Should we get out of here?"

"Solarian! Can I get a selfie with you?"

Ignoring them, I channeled my power, the intense heat of solar fusion, ready to unleash it. I stepped up to the truck, giving it a once over. It was black with garish green paint splattered over it. The windows were all closed, as were the doors. I leaned forward, listening for any hint of what was going on inside. Nothing.

I considered simply blasting the truck open, but I knew that wasn't an option. There was no telling how the doomsday weapon would react to a coronal blast. And it could've just been a falafel truck. No need for unnecessary property damage. So I rapped a knuckle against a window. "You guys opening anytime soon?"

Some folks behind me laughed. I tried to stay relaxed. A panicked crowd wouldn't help.

The window rolled up with an audible clank, and a Chinese man popped his head out. His eyes widened when he saw me. He stammered before finding his voice. "Sorry, we're not quite ready yet, uh...Solarian, sir. Been cooking all morning, but we're almost done."

I frowned. The man smiled, but he showed too much teeth. Beads of sweat trickled down his forehead. And I didn't smell anything coming from the truck.

Someone behind me screamed. I whipped around in time to see a picnic table flying at my head. I jabbed an open palm at it, incinerating it with a burst of solar radiation.

And there he was. The Baron. It was easy to see why he could blend into a crowd. In spite of his powers, he was wholly unremarkable. Average build, normal height. Graying hair, balding just a little. But there was no mistaking the hostile glee that burned in his eyes. I knew that at any moment he could transform into a monster.

"Ah, Solarian." His voice was gentle, almost soothing, but I could hear him over the shrieking crowd. "I did so hope you would be here today."

"Glad I didn't disappoint," I snapped. I clenched my fists and fire wreathed them. "Let's do this."

With a roar, I charged forward, slicing through the air toward my foe. The Baron didn't flinch. Instead, he smiled thinly. Then, right before I collided with him, he stepped to one side.

I should have sailed through the spot, but it felt like I had collided with a solid wall. An unseen force clamped onto my wrists and ankles and slammed me onto the pavement. No, not cement. A metal plate set into the pavement. A device of some kind? Clever trap, but it wouldn't be enough to stop me. I struggled, but try as I might, I couldn't break free. Okay, time to turn up the heat. But when I tried to unleash my power, the fire within me flickered and then went out.

My eyes widened. What was happening?

The Baron squatted down next to me. "I have so enjoyed our game of cat-and-mouse. But I tire of the drama." He reached into his coat pocket and pulled out a small remote, then pressed a big button in the center. "Inside that food truck is a bomb loaded with a kilogram of antimatter. It will detonate in five minutes. I know you could soak up the harmful radiation, but not while you're trapped in that dampening field, yes?

"Farewell, Solarian. The chase has been fun, but it ends today."

With that, he stood and calmly strode away. The crowd parted for him as he left. I twisted around to look at the falafel truck. The workers poured out of it, clearly panicked. But what could I do? I thrashed, but it was no use. I was stuck. Depowered. Done.

I collapsed onto the pavement, my chest heaving. I always knew there was a possibility of it all ending like this, but still. How could I have been so stupid as to walk into the Baron's trap? Now all these people were going to die, and that was on me. And I wouldn't even get to say goodbye to Clarissa.

Something metallic clanked onto the pavement. Then Tsuki kneeled down next to me. "Let's get you out of here."

I growled. "Don't worry about me. Evacuate the park. There's an antimatter bomb in the truck."

Tsuki glanced at the truck, then shook his head. "My sensors say the bomb's about to crit. There's no way we can get the crowd to a minimum safe distance in time. But if I free you, you could fly it safely away, yes?"

I pushed against the ground, trying to stand up, then collapsed. I nodded. "Probably. But what about the Baron?"

"You handle the bomb. I'll get the Baron."

I chuckled mirthlessly in spite of myself. "So you can get the glory."

"No, so we can save these people." Something clicked in Tsuki's helmet. And he spoke the next word without distortion. "Dad."

That voice! I'd know it anywhere. "No."

He—*she*—nodded. "Surprise."

Clarissa? My mind locked. She was only nineteen! She was supposed to be in college! When did any of this happen?

"Hold still." She flipped her wrist, and a small laser cutter popped out of her gauntlet. "Looks like the Baron has you trapped in a magnetic containment field with an inverted polarity loop. Clever, but..." Red light flared from the cutter and suddenly, I was free. "Now get the bomb out of here!"

I wanted to argue, but damn it, she was right. I whirled on the truck and sliced off the roof with a coronal beam. Then I leaped into the truck. The bomb was the size of a couch, lit up like the Vegas Strip, but thankfully, I could latch onto the casing. Still had to strain to lift the stupid thing. Definitely felt my age, but that couldn't stop me.

With a blast of power, I rocketed into the air, dragging the bomb with me. The city dropped away as I climbed, the air quickly getting thinner and colder. Had to have reached the edge of the atmosphere. I grunted as I spun the bomb around me, then tossed it as hard as I could straight up.

Not a moment too soon. The device dissolved in a flash of light. I opened my arms, trying to absorb as much radiation as I could. It burned through my veins. Probably didn't get all of it, but this far up, it hopefully wouldn't do much damage.

I flipped in midair and dropped back toward the festival. As I approached, I could see the crowd surging out of the Riverfront. Emergency personnel were on the scene, directing the chaos as best they could. But I could spot Clarissa fighting the Baron from five thousand feet up. Flares, laser blasts, and minor explosions dotted the ground. I grunted. No way that would penetrate the Baron's organic armor. I had to get in there and—

Wait. I stopped short, hovering in the air over the fight, and watched as my daughter took on her mother's murderer. And I saw.

She was brilliant.

In spite of the armor, Clarissa—no, *Tsuki*—moved with light-footed grace. Not a surprise, given the years of dance she had taken, but I doubt Madam Guiffre envisioned this sort of ballet. She flowed around the Baron, firing off small bursts of light to blind him. The villain had swelled to twice his normal size, his clothes in tatters. His armor had even grown spikes and sharp edges. I knew firsthand how durable he was when encased in that stuff. Even my strongest blast couldn't penetrate. But that didn't seem to bother Tsuki. She kept feinting and jabbing.

The Baron tried to give as good as he got. He ripped up pieces of cement and threw them at Tsuki, but he couldn't connect. At one point, he charged her and slammed into her midsection, but instead of going down, she flipped him over her hip and kept fighting.

Of course! Rather than try to overpower him, like I would have, Tsuki was tiring him out. And it worked. The Baron was slowing down. Showing his age. He wobbled, then stumbled to one knee, his chest heaving.

Tsuki looked up at me and motioned for me to land the finishing blow.

Oh, I wanted to. The power rose within me, an all-consuming inferno that yearned to be unleashed.

My lip twitched into a snarl. So easy.

But it wasn't my victory.

I landed gently. Tsuki cocked her head at me.

Shaking my head, I swept my arms toward the Baron. "This one's yours."

Tsuki chuckled, and with a mighty swing of her armored fist, knocked the Baron out.

Silence fell on the battlefield. Then pandemonium. The fleeing civilians flooded back into Riverfront, cheering for Tsuki. Reporters charged in after them. Within seconds, Tsuki was swamped with well-wishers and the press. She glanced over at me twice, but I shook my head and motioned for her to keep talking.

The impromptu press conference lasted until the eclipse itself. As the moon moved in front of the sun, an eerie pall fell over the Riverfront. The people surrounding Tsuki didn't even seem to notice.

And that was fine by me. After all, the sun isn't what makes an eclipse memorable. And it isn't the moon either. Instead, it's the two of them together that makes it so dazzling.

# NOTES ON "UPSTART"

CAN I JUST SHARE how much I enjoy the NYC Midnight Short Story Challenge?

I've been doing this contest for years now, and I always enjoy it. The way it works is simple. Each round, participants are assigned into heats. Each heat is assigned a genre, a subject, and a character. They then have to write a short story that incorporates all three within a certain length and with only so much time to work. With each successive round, the participants are given new prompts, but the time they have to write and how long the stories can be are both shortened. In the first round, participants are given approximately a week to write a 2,000-word short story. By the final round, the finalists have just 24 hours to write a 1,250-word short story.

I rarely make it past the second round. And I don't mind a bit. I always enjoy the challenge of getting the prompts and seeing what I can come up with. Sometimes it's easy. Other times, not so much.

*Upstart* was my first round entry for 2019. My prompts? An action-adventure about a fugitive and an eclipse. I remember being stumped until I realized that a superhero story is technically an adventure story. That realization put me firmly in the middle of my comfort zone. My debut novel was about a teenage superhero. As I thought it through, I realized the eclipse could be both literal and metaphorical. The story just fell into place.

Thankfully, the adventures of Solarian and Tsuki helped me move on to the next round, which is when I wrote...

# THE CALLS THAT HAUNT US

A LOT OF THINGS have haunted me in my life. Same as everyone, right? Missed opportunities, blown calls, deep regrets. But I never thought a literal ghost would haunt me.

Don't look at me like that, Doc. I know what you're thinking. Ghosts aren't real, right? Hell, I tried to explain it all away. When someone broke our porch lights and knocked over our trash cans, I figured it had to be some neighborhood kids. When someone yanked all the books off the shelves in my study, I promised Evelyn that I'd have a security system installed.

But then, one night, we woke up to what sounded like the house collapsing. The temperature dropped ten degrees and poor Staubach shot out of the room like his tail was on fire. As I reached for my gun, the noise stopped. Turns out someone had flipped over all of our furniture. The cops never figured out how they got in. When they saw the pics of me in my zebra shirt with Jerry Rice, Joe Montana, and Bud Grant and heard who I was, they came up with the same theory as me: some Falcons fans figured out where I lived and they were expressing their "displeasure" at That Call. Happened fifteen years ago, but some folks just can't let go. I bet you see that sort of thing a lot, right, Doc?

But Evelyn, she was convinced it was a ghost. And when she heard that Cesar Sandoval, the Bay Area Medium, was doing a Friday afternoon show at Mystic Lake, she got us tickets right away. Said it was a way to consult with an "expert."

Bunch of garbage, if you ask me. But Evelyn didn't, and I've learned over the past forty years that it's never a good idea to argue with her.

So there we were, front and center, crammed into the showroom with a ton of morons who had been rooked by Sandoval. I mean, seriously, how could anyone believe dead people would want to communicate through that greasy bag of hair? And yet they *oohed* and *aahed* as he pranced around in a shiny blue suit, his black hair gelled into a bouffant that would have made Patti LaBelle proud.

His eyes closed, he waggled his fingers toward the audience. "They want me to acknowledge...Mary. Does that mean anything to anyone tonight?"

Several people shouted that they had known Mary. I rolled my eyes and grumbled, but Evelyn elbowed me.

Sandoval spun some yarn about how Mary's fine, that the money would be taken care of, that they didn't have to grieve. And the audience ate it up, applauding like a bunch of trained seals.

He basked in the praise, pausing long enough to cough discreetly into a handkerchief. Then his eyes roamed the seats until they landed on...

Oh no.

Evelyn was waving frantically, like a kid who needed a hall pass for the restroom.

Sandoval kneeled down on the edge of the stage, a smarmy grin on his face. "Yes, ma'am? What can Sandoval do for you?"

A stagehand appeared at Evelyn's side and shoved a mic in her face.

"My husband and I are being haunted by some sort of spirit." Her voice was way too loud over the speakers.

She launched into her version of events, filled with evil poltergeists and shadows that hovered over our bed and crap like that. Sandoval didn't interrupt, although he did cough into the back of his hand a few times. But then he glanced at me, and it looked like maybe he recognized me. Wouldn't have surprised me. My face was all over the place after That Call and its aftermath. I got recognized occasionally, just a "Hey, aren't you Michael Baker?" sort of thing.

But I couldn't decipher the look Sandoval gave me. Hopefully, he wouldn't identify me.

Once Evelyn finished our tale of woe, Sandoval nodded sagely. "Well, that is quite the predicament, yes? Let us see if we can learn why the spirits are so angered."

He took a deep breath and closed his eyes. His head tipped to one side, then another, as if he were straining to hear something. I snorted. He was a great showman, I'll give him that, but—

Then Sandoval's body jerked. He went rigid, his arms snapping out. He coughed and black liquid sprayed from his mouth, then dribbled down his chin. Someone in the audience shrieked as he convulsed. As he did, the overhead lights exploded, showering glass and sparks. A blast of cold air swept over me, and invisible hands yanked me out of my seat, pulled up and over the edge of the stage and tossed at Sandoval's feet.

When I looked up, Sandoval hovered three feet off the stage, his jacket blowing in a breeze I couldn't feel. Then he looked down at me, and I gasped. His eyes had gone completely black, like empty holes.

He dropped to the stage and lurched toward me, like a marionette that was missing half its strings. "Michael Baker..." His voice was a wheezing growl.

Evelyn screamed, but I didn't look back at her. No way was I going to let this...this *thing* get to her. I scooted to one side so I was between Sandoval and her.

"Yeah, that's me. Who wants to know?"

Sandoval thumped himself in the chest. "Demarco."

My blood ran cold. Of course it would be him. Of course it would be because of That Call. I had been assigned to the 2005 NFC Championship game, the Eagles versus the Falcons. The Falcons were favored to win, mostly because of their rookie wide receiver, Demarco Woods. Anything Michael Vick threw, Demarco caught. Every single time.

Until Demarco got blindsided by an Eagles cornerback before he could catch the pass. Everyone was convinced that it had been pass interference, but that's not how I called it, because that wasn't how I saw it. Everyone blamed me when the Falcons lost. Folks called for my head. I got so many death threats that Evelyn and I had to move to Minnesota.

Things were worse for Demarco. His life fell apart. He went home to Kansas City during the off season, tried to forget what happened at the bottom of any bottle he could get his hands on. Wound up in a bar fight, the other guy pulled a gun, and that was it. A career with so much potential cut short. It was quite the scandal. Maybe you remember it? His face and mine were all over ESPN for weeks, but eventually folks moved on and most of them forgot about me.

But apparently Demarco hadn't.

I clambered to my feet and raised my hands. "Demarco... I'm sorry. But that was a long time ago and—"

Sandival—or was it Demarco?—threw his head back and howled. Some unseen force slammed into my chest and knocked me over again. I frantically rolled over, only to find Demarco looming over me.

"Sorry...not good enough," Demarco growled. It sounded like he was having trouble forming the words.

This didn't make sense. This all happened fifteen years ago. If he was going to haunt me, why wait so long? "But why come back now? You hate me that much?"

"Not hate. Love."

I froze. I wasn't sure how to take that.

Demarco crooked a finger at me. "Follow. Show you."

I glanced back at Evelyn. She had gone pale, but she shook her head.

"Um, I'm not sure that..." I started.

Demarco took a menacing step toward me, growling.

Now I know, Doc, it'd be crazy to go with him, right? But I figured, when a vengeful ghost is asking, you really can't say "No."

Nobody tried to stop us as we left Mystic. Not that I was too surprised. The whole casino was pandemonium. It was simple enough for Demarco and me to slip out of the building. Once we were on the road, Demarco only grunted directions to the other side of Minneapolis to some suburb called Columbia Heights. Seemed like a nice enough town. We drove up a hill to the high school, where a football game was starting up. I had to get the tickets. Demarco hung back, probably to hide the fact that something wasn't quite right with him. Thankfully, no one recognized either of us as we slipped into the stands.

"What are we doing here?" I asked.

No answer. I sighed. I guess that meant he wouldn't distract me from the game.

The announcer introduced the visiting team from South. Then he ran down the roster of the Columbia Heights Hylanders. The crowd went wild when he introduced a wide receiver, Kleavon Woods. I frowned. Woods looked pretty young. I asked one of the folks sitting nearby. Turned out he was a freshman, just called up from JV. That night was his varsity debut.

Demarco grunted as the guy gushed about how good Woods was, how everyone expected him to carry the Hylanders to state that season. "An NFL star in the making," he said.

I glanced at Demarco. "Is he why we're here?"

"Just watch."

Okay. I supposed that since I paid for the tickets, I might as well try to enjoy the game.

And it turned out pretty good. Minneapolis South put up a fight, but the Hylanders were too much for them, especially with Woods. The kid had the speed to carry him past the defense. And it seemed like whenever the quarterback launched a ball in his direction, Woods was right there to...

Wait a minute. I looked at Demarco. "Kleavon *Woods*? He's your son, isn't he?"

Demarco nodded slowly.

I turned back to the field. Woods caught another pass, a long bomb, but then the South defense took him down in the red zone.

"Is that why you haunted me? Just so you could see your kid play?" I asked.

Demarco shook his head. "No. Look."

Woods came out of the tackle hot. He went after one of the South players and got in the kid's face. It took three of his teammates to pull him back, but even then, it looked like he was ready to tear the other kid apart.

"Anger in him." Demarco turned to look at me with his dead eyes. "Don't want him on my path. Someone needs to teach him. Only a game."

My mouth went dry. Me? How was that supposed to work?

"Promise," Demarco whispered.

I stammered, wanting to deny it. Wanting to run out of the stands, call an exorcist. Or the Ghostbusters.

But as I stared at Demarco, I realized something. When we can make something right, we should. Right, Doc?

"Okay." The word slipped out of my mouth before I had really decided. But I nodded anyway. "I'll see what I can do."

I had no idea how to do what he wanted. How would I even introduce myself? *Hey, kid, I'm the guy who wrecked your dad's career. His ghost wants us to hang out. Wanna go get a milkshake?* But I had to try.

Demarco nodded once. "Thank you. Sorry about your house."

I laughed. "Don't worry. We'd been meaning to rearrange the furniture anyway. So...I suppose you're going to need to leave soon, huh?"

He nodded again. "Can't stay...much longer. Too hard."

I supposed it was. "How much time do you have? Enough to finish the game?"

Demarco smiled. "Let's see."

That crazy night's why I'm here, Doc. I know I promised you a ghost story, but I've been carrying baggage a lot worse than That Call and Demarco and never owned up to it. Those pains and regrets can haunt us worse than any ghost. Like I said, it's an even bigger mistake not to fix those problems. So what do you say, Doc? Where should we start?

# Notes on "The Calls that Haunt Us"

This story shoved me right out of that comfort zone. The prompts? A ghost story about a debut and a referee. What was I supposed to do with that?

I don't remember where I came up with the idea for "That Call." I seem to recall that something like this had happened in a game around the time of my writing this story. Or I ripped off this detail from the 2001 comedy *Rat Race*. That was enough to pull this together. The conversational tone felt right.

One other quick note: I sent Michael and Demarco to the town where I grew up. I used to sit in the same bleachers that they did when I played in the pep band. And yes, the mascot name, Hylanders, is spelled correctly. No, I don't know why we spelled it that way.

This was the end of the road for 2019. It turned out the judges didn't quite warm up to the story. That was all right, because as we went on to 2020, I was able to write one of my favorite stories ever...

# Hookah Jones and the Gas-Riders of Onrar

Millions of lives were at risk, so what was the delay?

That thought chased Korfa Fall as he paced the briefing room. His negotiation team was ready. The members of the Onraran Defense Force appeared to be too. Five burly men and women, dressed in blue fatigues, stood at relaxed attention, their faces impassive. If the tension was eating at them, they weren't letting on.

"I still don't understand why we can't take a skimmer." The question came from Seble Dia, who looked particularly uncomfortable in her enviro-suit. She kept tugging at the seams and sleeves, as if worried the protective fabric wasn't completely covering her. She didn't need to wear it inside the colony, but she insisted.

Fall's gaze drifted to the row of boards standing behind the soldiers. They were each three meters tall, made of gleaming metal. Unlike their terrestrial counterparts, these surfboards' undersides were dotted with vents and sensor nodes, designed to read the methane currents and feed info into the surfer's enviro-suit.

"As I explained to you already, ma'am, skimmers aren't safe on the al-Khwarizmi Straits," one soldier said. According to his ident tag, he was Captain Dymtrus Truss. "The interplay between the methane and the atmosphere creates dangerous crosswinds that will capsize skimmers. Not a problem on the boards."

Dia snarled at the explanation. She clearly wasn't suited for a fringer assignment like this, but she was a top diplomat for the United Terran Federation, so here she was.

Fall ignored her and quickly did the math. Five soldiers, five diplomats, five boards. They had what they needed, so what were they waiting for?

Hans Braaten, Fall's assistant, spoke up. "So why don't we get going? The native Onrarans were very clear: we have to be punctual. If we don't leave within the next ten minutes, we won't be. The talks could fail! Is that something you want on your conscience, Captain?"

Truss fixed Braaten with a withering stare. "You think I don't want peace? We've fought the gas-drinkers. I've lost friends to them. How many of you can say the same thing?"

Braaten bristled, and the other diplomats started muttering. The soldiers looked ready to fight. Fall winced. This could turn into a disaster if he didn't intervene.

He stepped between the soldiers and the diplomats. "I apologize for Mr. Braaten's insensitivity. We are just concerned about the delay."

Truss relaxed, but not by much. "We don't leave without Jones."

The other soldiers nodded. One of them said, "That's right."

Fall frowned. Jones? The UTF briefing said nothing about a "Jones" being involved. "Who's Jones?"

"Jones created this unit. He's the one who taught us how to surf the methane. He knows those seas better than anyone else. He's invaluable."

Oh. Fall looked over the assembled soldiers. If he had trained this obviously adept crew, then he easily would be an invaluable asset for the mission. But that left one question: "Then where is he?"

The door to the briefing room slid open, and an older man stumbled in. Fall couldn't help but stare. He looked as if he had been carved out of driftwood, his face wrinkled and gnarled. He wore a stained jumpsuit, badly patched in some places. His hair, a mass of white and black tangles, had been pulled into nearly a dozen braids. At the end of each braid was a wooden carving of birds, turtles, and other small animals. He looked around the room with bleary eyes before his gaze landed on Fall.

"You Fail?" he asked, his voice a long, loose drawl.

Fall bristled, standing up straighter. "I am Korfa Fall, Diplomat-at-Large for the—"

"Simple 'yes' woulda done it, my man." He stuck out a grimy hand. "Name's Hookah Jones. You ready to go?"

Fall gaped at the man. *This* was what they had been waiting for? Jones, who apparently didn't mind Fall's astonishment, walked up to the line of soldiers and hugged them one by one. Each soldier reciprocated with warm smiles.

"You boys and girls ready too?" Jones asked. "Looks like a good day to ride the waves, huh?"

"We're ready," Truss said.

Jones turned to the diplomats. "Fail, you're with Dim. The rest of you, partner up with one of these guys. We'll get you to the summit, don't you worry."

"We'd be less worried if you hadn't been so late," Braaten muttered.

Jones laughed. "Yeah, sorry about that. Last night, I took a double hit of dreamweave and I overslept."

Fall's mouth went dry. Their guide just openly admitted to using an illegal narcotic in front of government representatives. More maddeningly, the soldiers didn't seem to care. One of them actually chuckled and clapped the old man on the back.

Jones started for the exit. "Well, starshine's a-wasting. Gas-riders, let's surf!"

The soldiers grabbed their boards and followed Jones toward the airlock. Fall and the other diplomats watched them leave.

"We can't entrust this mission to that...that thing," Braaten whispered.

"Let alone our lives," Seble muttered.

Fall couldn't blame them for their hesitation. He didn't feel safe either. But...

He squared his shoulders. "My friends, we have a duty to the UTF, to peace, and to history. We have to see this through even if Jones is...unconventional. Please, let us see how this turns out."

The others didn't argue, but he could tell they wanted to. He couldn't blame them. But as he said, the mission was too important. Once they made it back, though, he would lodge a formal complaint with the UTF. Hookah Jones would be imprisoned or, better yet, exiled. There was no way Fall would allow that cretin to tarnish how history would remember him.

As the soldiers and diplomats emerged from the colony airlock, Fall couldn't help but stare. He had been briefed about Onrar's savage beauty. Seeing it firsthand, though, was something else.

A path led down to a glittering beach where liquid methane lapped against the shore. A dense fog hovered over the sea, pierced by large crystalline plinths that stabbed toward the dark sky. Stars shone brightly overhead, reflected as twinkling lights in the ocean by bits of crystal that floated in the sea.

Those crystals were the issue at hand. Lightweight and durable, they were perfect for crafting starship hulls. After UTF surveyors had discovered Onrar and its crystalline treasures, colonists flooded the planet hoping to get rich from crystal dredging. What no one knew was that the world was already inhabited, and the natives didn't take kindly to the humans' presence, resulting in open war for the past ten years.

Fall shook himself out of his reverie. Well, he was going to change that. He and his team would forge a lasting peace.

Someone bustled past him, carrying a piece of debris under their arm. Fall gaped at the intruder, wondering how a scavenger had made it into a military zone. But then he recognized the intruder's gait and height. Jones? The man wore an enviro-suit that looked as battered and badly patched as its owner. And his board! Unlike the soldiers' sleek metal boards, his looked like he had cobbled it together out of scraps! Fall took a moment to thank Allah he would not have to ride with him!

Truss appeared on his right. The helmet radio crackled. "Ready to go, sir?" Although Truss phrased it as a question, it clearly wasn't.

Fall nodded, and the two of them followed Jones down the path to the beach. The soldiers set their boards at the edge of the sea, then beckoned for their riders to join them. Truss helped Fall step up onto the board. As he did, he felt a vibration in his soles.

"Magnetic locks," Truss explained. "Just hold on to my shoulders and lean as I do."

"Yes, Captain."

Fall glanced down the line. The soldiers and diplomats looked ready. But Jones stood in the ocean, knee-deep, his board tucked under his arm. Jones dipped his left hand in the methane, then tossed it in the air where it vaporized almost instantly.

"What is he waiting for?" Braaten asked over the helmet comm.

"Cut the chatter," Truss snapped. "Jones knows the surf. We go when he says."

They waited, Jones squatting in the surf. Then, with a loud whoop that echoed in Fall's helmet and rattled his skull, Jones dove forward, tossing his board into the methane and hopping on. A wave swelled underneath him, and he shot off at incredible speed.

And then Truss's board surged forward, right behind Jones. Fall flailed, almost tipping over even though his boots were attached to the board. Truss reached back an arm and steadied him.

"Told you to hang on, sir," the captain said.

Chastised, Fall grabbed Truss's shoulders and leaned in. He glanced toward the others. The rest of the team clung to their surfers. He was pretty sure he heard Braaten whispering Hail Marys under his breath, but he couldn't tell for sure. Instead, he braced himself, thankful that they were finally on their way.

The sea wanted to murder them. That was the only explanation.

Winds slapped Fall from every direction. If it wasn't for the magnetic locks, he would have fallen off hours earlier. Lightning snaked through the sky, and the sea frothed, churning in larger and larger waves. Despite that, somehow Jones kept going. He didn't hesitate, leaping from wave to wave with wild cries of delight. The soldiers followed his lead and somehow they stayed together. But how Jones knew where to go was beyond Fall. Everything was chaos; the sea a featureless, frothing mass.

His stomach lurched as the board crested a wave and then dropped twenty feet.

"He's going to get us killed!" Fall muttered.

"Not today, sir," Truss replied.

Fall tightened his grip on the soldier's shoulders. Why had he agreed to this? Bah, he knew the answer. Glory! A place in the history books. The chance to make a mark on the UTF and its galactic policies. Oh, that had been a deceptive siren's call. And now he would die, drowned in methane, led to his death by...

He spotted Jones just ahead of them. Smoke burst from the vents on Jones's helmet, a sickly green mist that the wind snatched away.

Fall's jaw dropped open. "Is he still smoking dreamweave right now?"

Truss nodded. "Helps Jones read the waves, sir."

Fall spluttered as Jones twisted on his board, heading for...heading for...

Fall groaned. The waves ahead of them were even wilder, taller, and steeper. He screwed his eyes shut. Curse his pride! And curse Hookah Jones! At least they would die together!

Someone nudged Fall. "Sir? We're there."

Fall's eyes opened, and he realized the storm had ended. They jetted across the methane and there, in the middle of the roiling liquid, was a small island of crystalline sand, a blunt spike poking up out of the middle.

"Nipple Island, straight ahead!" Jones called.

"Wh-what?" Fall asked.

Truss shrugged. "Jones found it, so he named it. Kind of looks like a nipple if you squint."

Fall's stomach twisted. Would that be mentioned in the history books? Would the peace be named after the site? The Nipple Island Treaty?

Then he realized Jones wasn't slowing as he approached the island. He almost shouted a warning when Jones's board hit the beach, and he leaped off, landing with a spray of sand. He almost appeared graceful, but that was probably because he was so relaxed from the dreamweave.

Thankfully, the soldiers didn't imitate Jones's theatrics. They beached their boards gently and then helped the diplomats from their mounts. Fall's team stumbled onto the beach. Braaten collapsed onto his hands and knees, heaving. Was he vomiting into his suit? That would make the talks unpleasant,

The soldiers fanned out to the island's perimeter. Fall started for the plinth. According to his briefing, the UTF had paradropped shelters and supplies on the island already. Hopefully, it would last long enough. Fall expected the talks to last days, maybe longer. He'd probably have to call in for a resupply at some point.

But then the ocean on the far side frothed. Five large shapes rose out of the liquid.

They were the stuff of nightmares. Large, translucent green sacs ringed a head filled with black, beady eyes, more than a dozen of them, along with a twisted beak. Thin tentacles trailed down like hair, draped around a body that appeared to be a mass of shifting, pale seaweed. They almost looked like walking squids. Fall noticed metallic rings around their necks. He nodded to himself. According to the briefing, those would be translation and radio collars.

He forced himself to smile, even though the Onrarans couldn't see it, and stepped forward. "We are glad to be here with you today to—"

But the Onrarans shoved past him, rushing toward...

Fall sighed. Of course.

"Hookah Jones!" The warbly voice caused shivers to dance down Fall's spine. "We did not realize you would be here."

The Onrarans clustered around Jones, draping their tentacles over his shoulders and head, wrapping them around his waist. It almost appeared as if they were eating him. If only!

"Well, had to make sure these big-shots made it out here." Jones nodded in Fall's direction. "They've traveled a long way to end the hostilities."

"Yes, how they encroach on our seas and—" a new Onraran voice spat.

Fall took a breath to object, but Jones interrupted him.

"Now Kriich, they didn't know you was here. And you guys did attack first."

The Onrarans seemed to deflate. "You speak the truth."

"All they want is to talk about how you can all work together. You help them, they give you stuff, y'know?" Jones said.

"Cooperation is indeed our—" Fall said.

"Will it be a good agreement, Hookah?" one of the Onrarans asked.

Jones shrugged. "From what I've heard, yeah. They'll respect your spawning waters. And you don't even want them crystals, right?"

The Onrarans made strange chuffing sounds. Were they laughing?

"Then we agree."

Cold sluiced through Fall's veins so suddenly he worried his enviro-suit had breached. They *what*?

"If Jones says the terms are good, then hostilities will cease immediately," the Onraran continued. "Observe our borders and take the crystals."

"But—" Fall said.

The Onrarans rushed past him back into the sea, leaving the humans alone on Nipple Island.

"Well, that went well," Jones headed for the surf. "Let's get you back to the colony."

The soldiers also headed for the ocean. The diplomatic team stood there, transfixed.

"Sir?" Braaten asked weakly. "What the hell just happened?"

"I do not know," Fall said. He could already feel the weight of history falling from his shoulders. When this story was told to future generations, he knew he would only be a footnote, overshadowed by Hookah Jones.

# Notes on "Hookah Jones"

So where did this one come from? My first round assignment for 2020 was a comedy story about a surf instructor and a negotiation.

I had nothing. Absolutely nothing.

As I usually do, I went onto social media to complain. What could I possibly write about? But then my wonderful sister Becky had an interesting thought: "It doesn't specify location though." She followed that with a thoughtful emoji, an Earth emoji, and finally, a Saturn emoji.

She was right. Comedies can take place in outer space. I mean, my favorite television show of all time is *Mystery Science Theater 3000*. What if the surfer was on another planet? What if the negotiations were with aliens? What if the surf instructor was a stoned hippy in the future? It all just fell into place. I giggled the whole time I was writing it.

This was some of the most fun I had writing one of these entries. Well, for a while, anyway. There's another favorite coming.

But on to round two, right?

# A Small Step for Mama T

I glared at the monsters. They appeared impassive, but I knew if I let my guard down, they'd devour me. That's why, every time I stood in front of them, I established my dominance. They had to know who was in charge.

One of them, DeMarcus King, leaned over to whisper something to his neighbor. Probably thought I couldn't see the back of the room.

"King!" I raised my voice just enough that it was loud but not a shout.

He sat bolt upright in his desk, his eyes wide.

"What's rule number one in my class?"

King stammered. "No talking unless called on."

"And you were...?"

"...talking."

I nodded. "That's a detention."

A murmur rippled through the class. That wasn't the way my colleagues did things. Most would give a warning. But these kids needed a firm hand. They had to learn there would be consequences to their actions, and they would thank me one day.

But from the way most of them glared at me, that day wouldn't be today. Not a surprise. I'd have an easier time finding Bigfoot than a thirteen-year-old who actually respected authority. They were too full of hormones and hopped up on

TikTok and other garbage to think straight. Especially since it was a Friday and they could smell the weekend approaching.

"Does anybody have a problem with that?"

Nobody did. I nodded to myself. Then it was time to get to work.

I spent the next twenty minutes trying to shove knowledge into their brains, namely how to write a haiku. I sighed. I hated poetry. Reading it, teaching it, listening to the garbage these kids would inevitably cook up. But the curriculum said I had to, so here I was, explaining the whole 5-7-5 structure to kids who probably couldn't count that high without the help of Siri.

Once I had done my level best, I set them loose to work on their own haikus. And, to their credit, most of them did. They hunkered down, scribbling away. I surveyed the room, my arms crossed. I was even tempted to smile, but I knew that would only backfire on me.

Someone knocked gently at the door. I glanced over and swallowed a wince. Gita Kaur, the principal, beckoned me from the door. I sighed, already knowing why she had come all the way up to my room. Might as well face the firing squad.

"Keep working." I headed for the door. "What can I do for you, Ms. Kaur?"

"Mr. Erickson, I just heard from Holly Tomlin's parents. Did you really give her detention for looking at her phone?" From her tone, Gita already knew the answer.

I stood up straighter. "Policy is phones are shut off and in the lockers while school is in session, right?"

"Well...yes."

"And Holly broke that rule."

"But she's an honor roll student, never had any trouble before."

"Then maybe this will make sure that—"

Glass shattered behind me. I rushed back into the room. The students all sat there, wide-eyed, most of them staring at my desk. I turned and saw what had caused the noise. A picture frame had toppled off my desk. Broken glass was scattered across the floor.

I rushed to the frame and picked it up. My parents smiled up at me, their features warped through the cracks. My fingers tightened around the frame.

This had been my great-grandmother's, passed down to each successive generation when they graduated high school. And the picture was from my parents' funeral, but that appeared intact. Only the glass appeared broken.

But how had the frame fallen? I made sure it was never near the edge of my desk. If this fell off...

My eyes snapped up to my students. Several of them had gone pale. They knew what kind of storm was coming. Time to bring some thunder.

"Who did this?" I whispered.

No answer. Some of them had the audacity to look away.

"Who did this?" I roared.

Misty Clearbottom, seated in the front row, squeaked. "N-n-no one, Mr. Erickson. It just fell on its own."

"No," I spat. "Someone did this. King! Was this you?"

The fear painted across his face was answer enough, but he still shook his head. No, I supposed he couldn't have made it up to my desk and back to his seat so quickly.

"Well, someone did. And either you tell me who it was, or I'm giving all of you detention!"

"Mr. Erickson!" Geta's voice cut through the gasps. "Are you sure that's necessary?"

I held out the picture frame. "This is an antique, Ms. Kaur. And someone broke it. And I want to know who. Now!"

Even as I stared fire at them, no one had the courage to 'fess up. I waited a few minutes, then whirled on Geta.

"Fine. Ms. Kaur, I hope you have a big enough room. I want these..." I caught myself before I cursed. "...students to have detention starting Monday until one of them tells the truth."

"But I was telling the truth, Mr. Erickson! It fell over on its own, just tumbled right off the desk!" Misty looked ready to cry.

"I'll double it!" I said.

That put an end to the arguments. Ms. Kaur tried half-heartedly to talk me out of it, but she knew she couldn't. My mind was made up. And the rest of the class finished in blissful silence. I had made my point. No one doubted my authority after that.

When I opened the door to my apartment, cold air crashed over me. I could practically see my breath as I made it to the thermostat, where I discovered the temperature was…68? I frowned, and suddenly realized that the chill that had chased me down the hall was gone. I frowned. That was weird. I tried to find a draft but came up short. I made a note to talk to the super about it and settled in to eat my takeout dinner.

Halfway through, though, the entire room started shaking. The pictures rattled on the walls, and I was sure that every dish I owned would tumble out of the kitchen cupboards. I braced myself for the ceiling to collapse, but just as quickly as it started, it ended. Once I knew it had stopped for sure, I dashed to the window and looked outside, expecting to see a convoy of semis roaring by at top speed. The streets were empty. And it didn't sound like my neighbors were panicking. Everything seemed perfectly normal.

I stepped back into the apartment and frowned. What was going on?

Thankfully, the rest of the evening passed uneventfully, and finally, I clambered into bed and drifted off to sleep.

I was jolted awake when my bed started rattling. The same sub-zero chill fell upon me, and I was suddenly aware of a shadow that loomed over my bed. I scrambled away from it, bumping against the wall.

"It's good to see you again, Clarence."

My jaw dropped open. I knew that voice. "Mama T?"

The shadow dissolved to reveal the smiling face of my great-grandmother. Mama T was an Erickson legend, a mother of seven kids, most of whom she raised on her own when her husband died of the flu. She had been a fixture at every graduation, every wedding, every family reunion, every funeral. She looked just the way I remembered her: short, stocky, wearing enough shawls to crush a normal person. Normally, I would have been thrilled to see her.

Except she had died thirty years ago.

I closed my eyes and shook my head. "I have to be dreaming."

Pain exploded across the side of my head as if someone had slapped me.

Mama T smiled sweetly, then sighed deeply, and she shook her head sadly. "What happened to you, Clarence?"

"I-I'm not sure what you mean."

"Where's the boy I knew? Do you remember when the family all got together in Mobile back in '78?"

Vaguely. My mind flooded with images of giants looming over me, dozens of kids running around. And, of course, Mama T holding court at one end of the pavilion.

"Remember what happened when Petey spiked that volleyball into Tanya's face?"

I stared at her blankly.

She chuckled. "Well, I do. Everyone freaked out. But you just plopped down next to Tanya and started crying. You weren't hurt. You were just upset that she was. What happened to that sweet little boy?"

I still had no idea what she was talking about, but it opened up a chasm in my chest. What changed me? I grew up alone. My parents both died while I was in college. And then Pauline left me. I had to be strong and independent from such an early age.

Mama T clucked her tongue. "I didn't want to believe what I was seeing. That's why I knocked over that picture frame today."

My head snapped back as if I had been struck. "That was you? But why?"

"A test. I wanted to see your reaction. Such anger and vitriol. Is that really what those kids need most? How do you think they'll turn out if they keep getting smacked down for any little thing?"

"They'll be stronger, more disciplined, able to focus. More like me."

"And is that as great as you think it is?"

Her quiet question stung.

"Maybe not."

Mama T put a hand on my chest. "I know that big-hearted boy is in there. Maybe let him out once in a while?"

I swallowed hard and nodded. I could. It wouldn't be easy. I had twenty years of momentum shoving me down this path. But maybe with little nudges, I could try.

"Good! And don't worry. I'm never that far from you."

Then her body dissolved, like a sand pillar being blown away by a gentle breeze, leaving me alone.

But not lonely. And filled with thoughts about how things could be better.

Monday, when third hour English filed into my room, I could feel the tension they carried with them. They didn't speak as they took their assigned seats. I could practically taste the fear in their expressions and postures.

I sighed as the bell rang. I levered out of my chair and walked around my desk. "'The light of a candle / Is transferred to another candle— / Spring twilight.' Yes, that was a haiku, written by master poet Yosa Buson." I looked down at the floor. "I've been so focused on trying to pass the light of a single candle that I forget that you are all spring twilight. You've all got bright futures ahead of you. And I thought I was helping. But I realize I've been dimming that light."

I studied their faces again. Skepticism. Confusion. Uncertainty. They probably thought I had lost my mind.

"I'm still going to expect you to be respectful and to do your work. But I'm also going to do my best to let you guys shine. So get out your haikus, okay?" I started for my desk, but then caught myself. "And that detention you all owe me? None of you need to worry about it anymore. That goes double for you, Mr. King."

Quiet celebration swept through the room, and they got to work. As the students pulled out their assignments, I returned the picture frame to the corner of my desk. Over the weekend, I replaced the glass, but I also replaced the picture. Instead of my parents' funeral picture, it was of us at the 1978 family reunion in Mobile. My folks, smiling and happy, with me in between them, tear tracks on my cheeks. And there was Mama T, hugging me close.

"I'll do my best, Mama T," I whispered. Then I looked up at my students. "Let's see what light you've got to share."

# Notes on "A Small Step for Mama T"



Another ghost story? Really?

That it was a ghost story about detention and a matriarch? That made it even worse. I fought this one. I struggled with it. The details about Clarence sitting down next to an injured Tanya was inspired by something my oldest did in preschool. And it turned out that I just can't do ghost stories. It's not my thing. The judges noticed that as well. This was the end of the road for me that year.

The ironic thing is that, when I wrote this story, I was still a Lutheran pastor. But I realized, as I compiled this anthology, I'm now the English teacher who doesn't always enjoy teaching poetry. I haven't been haunted by any of my ancestors yet, but I suppose I'm still pretty new to teaching.

# A ROLL OF THE DICE

THE SPINNING BOTTLE RATTLED. With each clink, Connor's stomach twisted tighter. This was not what he expected to do at the party. Watch his classmates get drunk, sure. Watch them make fools of themselves? Probably. But play a mash-up of spin the bottle and truth or dare? Not even a possibility.

His gaze skipped to Mike's face. The party's host smiled lazily. When Mike caught Connor sneaking into the party, he hadn't tossed him out. Instead, he and his girlfriend, Staci, gathered half a dozen others to play this homebrew truth or dare. And he couldn't refuse. Not if he wanted to complete his quest.

The bottle slowed. Connor grabbed handfuls of his jeans, offering a silent plea. *Please, not me. Not again.*

But apparently fate didn't care. With one last clatter, the bottle pointed at him.

Mike leaned forward to speak, but Staci laid a hand on his arm and asked, "Well, Connor? Truth or dare?"

He resisted the urge to glare at her. She already knew the answer. According to her rules, you couldn't pick the same option twice in a row. Since he had already picked truth, he had to choose: "Dare."

Staci's smile turned predatory. "You know Neala, right?"

Neala sat next to Staci. She stared at the bottle with intense green eyes, her blond hair framing her pretty face. Did he know her? Neala, who sat in front of him in English? Neala, whose bright laughter haunted his thoughts at inopportune times? Neala, who he had hoped he'd be able to talk to at this party? Yes, he knew her.

"Well, I have a special task for you to do...together," Staci's words were laced with innuendo.

Neala's cheeks flushed, and a pit opened in Connor's stomach. Something thudded into his lap. He looked down and frowned. Why had Staci thrown a video camera at him? Did she expect them to make a sex tape?

"Here's what you're going to do." Staci's voice was a sultry purr. "You're going to take that camera, and then you and Neala are going to go across the street and find proof of what Mr. Nellis is."

Sweet relief flooded through Connor. He had thought Staci intended them to make out or have sex or something like that. But then Staci's actual words caught up to him, and the twisting in his stomach turned into a consuming void. He considered bailing right then and there. But then he met Neala's gaze, and his anxiety lessened. After all, there was no way that their principal was actually a serial killer, right?

Connor tried to keep his head held high as he and Neala crossed the street toward the mortal remains of Anne Etheridge High School. In the darkness, the building looked every inch a haunted keep. Anne Etheridge had been closed for as long as he could remember. Most of the kids got bused to Southridge now.

And so did Mr. Thomas Nissel, who got promoted from vice principal to "the big chair." Connor had never really interacted with Nissel. But he had definitely heard the stories: Nissel was a serial killer with a secret killing room in Anne Etheridge and a body count in the dozens or maybe more. The stories were ridiculous, but Connor understood why people believed them. Nissel had always creeped him out, with his intense gaze and soft-spoken voice.

Neala paused in the middle of the street. Connor could practically feel the uncertainty boiling off her.

"So, are we really doing this?" he whispered.

She shrugged. "There's nothing to be scared of, right?"

Someone hooted behind them. He risked a glance over his shoulder. Mike, Staci, and some of the others were watching. He forced himself to turn back to the school. All the windows and doors on the first floor had been boarded up. The second floor, too. A few windows were broken on the third floor, but he had no idea how they'd get up there.

"So how do we get in?" he whispered.

"Staci says there's an open door around back."

Oh. Somehow it didn't surprise Connor that Staci knew that

"C'mon, let's go." Neala gently pushed him forward.

Connor almost tripped over his feet at the touch. A few of the guests shouted suggestions where he should touch her back.

Neala scowled over her shoulder. "Sorry about that."

"It's okay." How he got the words out of his suddenly dry mouth was a mystery.

She regarded him. "You know, I was surprised to see you here tonight."

"Why's that?"

"This doesn't seem to be your kind of thing."

"Oh? And what would my 'thing' be?"

She shrugged. "I don't know. Playing D&D in someone's basement?"

Was it that obvious? Yeah, that was what he had wanted to do, but Kevin had dared him to crash Mike's party. When Kevin dangled the prize in front of him, Connor knew he had no choice.

Thankfully, she led the way around the building. Sure enough, an unlocked door led to a locker room. Dust and rust covered everything. The smell of mildew and old sweat caused Connor to gag.

"So, what's the plan?" he asked.

Staci nodded at the camera. "We'll just head to the principal's office. Then we'll head back to the party and admit defeat. Easy."

The confidence in her voice bled into Connor, and he stood a little straighter. Sure. Easy as anything.

Turned out, not easy. While Neala and Connor found their way into the main part of the school, folding security gates blocked many of the halls, creating a maze. As they made their way through the darkened hallways, they passed by decaying classrooms. With every step, Connor wanted to run.

But Neala didn't seem nearly as worried, and so he soldiered on.

After wandering through the maze, they came to a stairwell.

"Maybe we can find a way around the gates if we use the stairs?" Neala asked.

He motioned for her to lead the way while he kept filming. She descended into the school's basement.

Thankfully, none of the security gates in the basement were shut. But the mood was even more oppressive and dank. A sign offered directions to shop classrooms and the weight room, but it was askew, the arrows pointing to the floor and the ceiling. Connor's heart hammered, and he backpedaled a step. This felt too dangerous, too risky. Was the building even safe? Could it collapse on them?

Neala snared his hand and gave it a little squeeze. "You okay?"

He met her gaze, and he saw his own nervousness reflected in her eyes.

"Fine," he lied. Both to her and for her.

They continued past more vacant classrooms and unlabeled doors. Connor's nose wrinkled as unfamiliar smells assaulted him. Instead of mold and dust, now he smelled...sulfur? Were they near a chemistry lab? Maybe the school's basement contained a portal to Avernus. He chuckled at the ridiculous thought. Why would a doorway to the Nine Hells be here?

But then he spotted a dim red dot of light along one wall. He stooped down. A baby monitor? He frowned. It looked relatively new and clean. Why was *this* here? The portal to Avernus would make more sense.

Neala motioned for him to keep moving. Connor picked up the pace. If they could find the cafeteria, maybe there would be stairs nearby. Hopefully, they'd find a way to the office and then...

Something clattered in the distance.

Connor froze. The sound had been so sudden; had he imagined it? Neala's eyes were wide and her chest heaved. So he snared her hand and gave it a squeeze. They exchanged fearful looks, and then she stepped forward, pulling him along. And he followed, just glad for the anchor of her grip in the midst of this stupidity.

The sulfuric smell grew stronger. And the darkness gave way to flickering lights. Was anyone else in the building? Mike and Staci, maybe? Was this an elaborate prank leading to a jump scare? Was Neala in on it?

Neala didn't wait for him, peeking into what turned out to be the cafeteria. A row of tables were covered with glass beakers, propane tanks, and torn-apart cardboard boxes. Three rough-looking men hunched over the makeshift chemistry lab. Connor gritted his teeth. He had seen enough episodes of *Breaking Bad* to recognize a meth lab.

One worker looked up and spotted them. The gnarled man's face twisted. "Hey!"

Connor dragged Neala out of the cafeteria, dropping the camera as he ran. Back down the hall, trying to find a way out. He could hear the men running after them, closing in.

There! Stairs. Connor urged Neala to hurry, taking two at a time himself. At the landing, they almost ran headlong into a stack of desks. Connor grabbed one and yanked, sending them tumbling down the stairs in a loud clatter. Based on the yelps and shouts, it sounded like he might have hit someone.

They burst onto the main floor. There had to be an exit nearby. But the main floor was still a maze. Connor kept moving, darting down different hallways, keenly aware that their pursuers were gaining.

He skidded to a halt. Exit doors, right in front of them, but chained shut. He winced. Not good. He turned to run back the way they had come, only to realize the men had caught up.

"Whatsa matter, kids?" one of them asked. "Lookin' pretty scared there."

Connor stepped between the men and Neala. He knew he couldn't fight them off, but at least he could offer her a little protection. Maybe. "We don't want any trouble. If you just let us go, we'll—"

"Not how this works."

Connor put up his fists, but the men clearly didn't feel threatened. They laughed as they advanced.

And then suddenly, one of them was down, howling and clutching at his knee. What happened? Then Connor realized there was a fourth man swinging a baseball bat. A second man went down. Their rescuer spun, catching the last man in the chest. In a matter of heartbeats, it was all over.

Their rescuer turned to Connor. Connor's mouth popped open.

"Mr. Nellis?" he asked.

Their principal held out a hand. "C'mon, let's get you two out of here."

Not surprisingly, Mike, Staci, and the rest of the party were long gone before the cops showed up. The neighborhood was bathed in flashing red and blue lights. Connor stared at Mike's house numbly. This wasn't how tonight was supposed to go. Neala seemed just as out of it as he felt. He vaguely listened as Mr. Nissel explained to the police how he had just been in the neighborhood, saw Mike's party and realized something must have been happening in the old school, and investigated. The police seemed upset about Mr. Nissel putting himself in danger, more so since the lab workers had apparently escaped. Connor disagreed. Who knew what would have happened if Mr. Nissel hadn't been there?

Connor glanced at Neala. "Are you okay?"

She shrugged, then gestured vaguely toward Mike's house. "Glad to see my friends made sure I was okay. Makes me wish I hadn't come."

"Same."

"So why did you? No offense, but I don't think you were invited."

His cheeks flushed. "You're right. I wasn't."

"So..." She made a prompting motion.

He sighed. Might as well cap off the night with a little humiliation. "My friends dared me to crash Mike's party."

She laughed. "I hope you're getting something good out of it."

He screwed his eyes shut. He didn't want to see how she'd react to this. "They said if I made it in and stayed for the entire party...they'd give me 35,000 experience points for my rogue."

Silence. It dragged on so long that he eventually risked a peek.

Neala gaped at him. "35,000—"

"—experience points. You weren't wrong about D&D."

"Oh." She tapped a fist against her thigh. "Bet you wished you had done that tonight instead, huh?"

"Yeah." He considered her. Why not take one more risk? "You know...you could join us if you want."

Neala studied him, then smirked.

He steeled himself for the rejection. He should have known better than to ask.

"Only if your friends are okay with me playing a Tiefling Circle of Dreams druid."

Well, Benny played a druid, but he supposed they could make it work if...

Wait, *what*?

She smiled. "I'd love to. Maybe next time, our dungeon crawl won't end like this, huh?"

A laugh bubbled up his throat. Maybe the risks had been worth it. Maybe sometimes you just had to roll the dice.

Mr. Nissel watched as the last police car pulled away from the school. He forced himself to keep his mask in place: the easy-going smile, the friendly wave, the relaxed posture. No telling how long he'd be observed. This was a close one, no doubt. Too close. He'd been too negligent, too sloppy, to allow this.

As the police disappeared into the darkness, Nissel marched back into Anne Etheridge. With each step, the disguise fell away. First the smile. Then, the relaxed gait. Anne Etheridge demanded his true self. She always had.

He reviewed the story he had told the police. He thought his performance went well. While he could read the cops' skepticism, Connor and Neala's babbling account of what happened lent his version credence. He smiled tightly. Gullible, the lot of them.

Nissel relaxed as soon as he stepped through the door. Anne Etheridge. His lady. His sanctuary. Southridge couldn't compete with all the cameras and scrutiny and questions.

He navigated the maze of corridors to the basement to the old auto shop. To a casual observer, the door appeared welded shut, but if someone knew the secret, it was easy enough to open. Nissel knew the secret. He was the one who made the secret.

Once the door had scraped open, he stepped inside and switched on the generator. The work lamps flickered to life, revealing his inner sanctum: the wall of mementos, his waiting tools, the tables for his friends.

He stepped into the light, and his three new friends squirmed, trying to plead through the gags. He sighed. They weren't his type. He had exacting specifications for his friends. But these three had violated his beloved Anne Etheridge. Endangered her. And him. They were friends, but only out of necessity, so he wouldn't enjoy this as much. He couldn't afford to.

Nissel offered his new friends a tight smile. "Let's begin."

Much to his delight, despite his initial misgivings, Nissel found he could enjoy himself with these friends. Ah, Anne Etheridge. She never ceased to amaze him.

# Notes on "A Roll of the Dice"

New year, new prompts. For round one in 2021, I was assigned a thriller about a principal and a dare.

So where did this story come from? At the time, I was listening to a Dungeons and Dragons podcast created by some online friends of mine. Originally called "Dungeon Drunks," it eventually became "Distinguished Adventurers." They were in the middle of a multi-year campaign that was an absolute blast. That gave the seed for Connor's dare and the way things resolved with Neala.

Another inspiration was my childhood home. We lived kitty-corner across the street from Nelson Elementary School, which I attended through first grade. But after first grade, the school closed and was boarded up for years. When I was a child, we would often head over there and walk around the block. I remember sneaking up to the windows and looking through them at classrooms that still had desks in them. There were so many times I wished I could have explored the interior of Nelson. I was sure that there would be treasures to find and adventures to be had. I never worked up the nerve to try, and I never got the chance. The school was eventually turned into condominiums.

So what about the ending? I love a good twist. There's a reason *Empire Strikes Back* is my favorite movie. That's why I decided that the rumors about Mr. Nissel were true. I thought that would be fun.

The judges disagreed. 2021 was one and done.

# THE HOME HE BUILT

THEY CALLED IT "SUNNYSIDE," but this shouldn't be anyone's home.

The odor of stale urine mixed with desperation assaulted Lee. Residents slumped in wheelchairs, either staring at nothing or lifting pleading eyes toward him. Lee shuddered. How could anyone live here?

But he didn't know anyone's circumstances. Maybe they couldn't afford better. Maybe they didn't have anyone watching out for them. Or maybe they had a jerk son-in-law who didn't care where she wound up.

Lee grimaced as he stepped into room B-104. Those thoughts weren't helpful. He plastered on what he hoped was a caring smile. Paula deserved that at least.

The room was cramped with too much furniture for two people. Sunlight trickled through a smudged window. Mrs. White didn't seem interested in the view. Instead, she mumbled as she stared at the ceiling. In Lee's memory, Mrs. White was an exuberant woman, quick to scold but just as quick to laugh at the neighborhood kids. But now, she appeared only a fading echo.

Paula sat next to the bed, and the similarity between the two women drew Lee up short. She had always resembled her mother, but now they both wore the same haggard expression.

"I'm sorry to bother you..." Lee said.

Paula checked on her mother, then smiled, a tired twist of her lips. "Weren't you going to the house?"

"I was, but Matt texted me. He doesn't have the key, so..."

Irritation flashed through Paula's eyes, but she rummaged in her purse. As she did, Lee kneeled next to Mrs. White's bed.

She kept mumbling the same thing. "Want to go home. Call you home."

Lee grimaced. If he lived here, he'd want to go home too.

"Good to see you, Mrs. White," he whispered. "You hang in there, okay?"

That caught her attention. She reached for him. "Benji? Did you get the groceries in?"

A pang shot through his chest. Benji was Paula's brother and his best friend growing up. Only he died fifteen years earlier.

"Take it as a compliment," Paula whispered. "Half the time she doesn't know me."

The pain in Paula's voice stung him too. Losing her brother, then her dad, and with her mom fading like this...

Mrs. White looked back toward the ceiling and murmured about going home again. Paula held out a house key.

"You need anything else?" she asked.

Nothing he could have asked for, like answers or hope or comfort, was for him. Those would all be for her. He shook his head.

"I'll see you later." She resumed her vigil at her mom's side.

Lee paused in the doorway, taking in the drab room one more time. No, this should be no one's home.

It looked like the Whites' home hadn't changed at all. Still nestled in a cul-de-sac, surrounded by stately trees, the house appeared frozen in time.

But as he drew closer, he spotted the signs of decay. The window screens were torn and dirty. The siding was rotten or needed paint. And it looked like the foundation had cracks. He winced. Seeing this would have broken Mr. White's heart.

So where was his brother? His car was in the middle of the driveway, making it impossible for anyone else to park there. But Matt was nowhere to be seen.

"Matt?" Lee called.

As he walked around the house, he realized the gate leading to the backyard was open. He slipped through and sure enough, there was Matt, yakking on his cellphone.

"... in-laws' place, yeah." He clearly didn't care that his voice carried. "No one's lived here since Paula's pop died, and it is a wreck. I have no idea how much we'll get out of it... Well, I don't have time and Paula's been no help. So I got my kid brother to do it. He needs some extra cash after that bar of his went belly up."

Heat flashed through Lee's chest. How long was Matt going to hold that over him? Sure, he would never be as successful as Matt, but he had done okay for himself. And how could he have known the pandemic would end things so abruptly? It wasn't his fault he had to move in with Mom and Dad again.

But no, he wouldn't start that fight now. Mom, always plugged into the gossip in the old neighborhood, had told him how much Mrs. White had struggled after Mr. White passed. He had apparently been making up for her decline for a while. No one had realized until he was gone. After the funeral, Mom had promised Mrs. White and Paula that she would help any way she could. So when Paula and Matt needed someone to clean out the Whites' house, Mom had volunteered Lee. Then Matt had turned it into a charitable handout.

Matt spotted him by the gate. "Gotta go. Lee finally showed up." He tucked his phone away. "You got the key?"

Lee held them up. Matt jerked his head toward the back door and headed that way without checking to see if Lee was following. When they reached the door, Matt snapped his fingers and held out his hand. Lee sighed. As if he didn't know how to work a lock.

Once they were in, a musty odor assaulted him, not as strong or as bad as the nursing home, but enough to make him pause.

"Yeah, we're going to have to do some deep cleaning after you're done. Emily left a mess before we got her into the home." Matt tromped up the stairs and into the kitchen.

Lee followed, looking at the full garbage bags stacked on the steps. The kitchen wasn't much better, with half the cupboards open and stacks of random dishes piled on the counters.

"We need you to sort through everything. We've got a dumpster coming this afternoon for the trash. I think Paula wants you to save the furniture, but I don't really care. We don't have room for much in our place." Matt pulled some money out of his pocket. "Mom said you needed some help, so here you go. Thanks, man, I appreciate it."

With that, Matt left the house, leaving Lee standing in a dank kitchen with three hundred dollars and a monumental task ahead of him.

There was a closet stuffed with plastic bags. There had to be hundreds of them, all squished together so tightly none budged when he opened the door. Lee stared at the wall of white plastic and sighed. Yet another mess.

Actually, the house wasn't that bad. Some spots were worse than others. Mrs. White's chair in the living room had stacks of unpaid bills and old advertisements. Towels and sheets in the master bedroom never got put away. And the bathroom... well, Lee had decided early on that he'd leave that for the professionals who came after him.

He spent the first couple of days working through the first floor. Some rooms were easier than others. Benji's old room, for example, had already been stripped years earlier. Now all that was left was a double bed and an empty bookshelf dotted with some of his old knickknacks. And apparently Mr. White had been using Paula's room before he passed; his things were neatly tucked away in the dresser and closet. Little of Paula remained, save for faded wallpaper and a few scribbled words on the inside of the closet door.

The tedious work gave him time to think. In many ways, he could identify with the Whites' house. His life had been crumbling for the past two years. Sure, his bar never impressed Matt, but it had been *his*. He had figured out how to run that business his way. But now that it was gone, he didn't know what to do with himself or his life. It felt like trash just kept piling up in random corners of his life, threatening to overwhelm him. So it felt good to carry each load of trash out to the dumpster. At least he was making progress there.

Once he had finished with the first floor, Lee turned his attention to the basement. As he descended the steps, nostalgia swept away his mind. How many times had he and Benji slammed down those steps?

The basement was largely how he remembered it: the same brown carpeting, wood paneling, hand-me-down couches. Lee lingered at the bottom of the steps, soaking in the memories. Benji and their friends staying up late into the night playing *Street Fighter.* Or sneaking down here to spy on Paula and her friends during a sleepover.

Lee moved along one wall, not wanting to break the memories. He ran one hand along the paneling, feeling the uneven nails. When the Whites bought the house, the basement had been unfinished. When he was a kid, Lee and Benji would come down here to play. The bare cement floors and walls were the perfect backdrop for their adventures as knights. But when Paula entered middle school, Mr. White finished the basement on his own. He hadn't been a carpenter—Lee never really understood what he did for a living—but he had been willing to figure out the basics on his own. Mr. White and Dad had spent weeks down here, drinking beers and laughing while they made stupid mistakes mudding drywall and helping other friends who knew how to do things like wiring and plumbing. The result wouldn't win any beautiful home awards, but when he was a kid, Lee didn't care. And he didn't mind so much now either.

He came across the Whites' pride wall, dotted with pictures of their kids. Benji mugged in most of them, but in the final one, he looked grim in his new

Marine uniform. And then there was Paula, smiling and bubbly. Lee glanced over her prom pictures. He couldn't remember the names of her dates in the first two, but when he saw Matt standing behind her for their senior prom, he felt the usual jealous pang. Just like when he was younger, he momentarily pictured himself in Matt's place, but he shoved the old feelings away. Old water under a dangerous bridge crossed too long ago.

A door tucked in one corner took him into Mr. White's workshop. Lee could picture Mr. White hunched over his workbench, trying to figure out how to fix a toaster oven or glue a leg back onto a chair. There was a lot of trial and error, but Mr. White had always said it was worth it. "If you love something enough, you'll figure out how to make it work," had been his mantra.

Lee crossed over to the row of cabinets that lined one wall. Again, Mr. White had cobbled them together, so the doors were a bit crooked and the individual cabinets were slightly different sizes. One by one, Lee opened them, revealing boxes of books, mementos, clothing. But in the last one, he was surprised to find an old, banged-up guitar case.

He pulled it out and dusted it off. Whose was it? Benji had never played. Neither had Paula. He popped it open. The guitar itself appeared to be in good shape. Lee hadn't touched one in years. He had pawned his in a last-ditch effort to save his bar. But he gingerly picked up the guitar and gave the strings a quick strum. Out of key, but that was easily fixed. Whoever owned this guitar had taken good care of it.

Tucked into a pocket in the case were loose papers and black-and-white photos. Lee checked the pictures first. They were all of Mr. and Mrs. White when they were teenagers, laughing and hugging and kissing. And the last one was of Mr. White playing a guitar while Mrs. White stared at him dreamily. And the papers? Chords and words, scribbled through and written over. Mr. White had written music? Lee couldn't imagine that. But here was the evidence: dozens of pages of cobbled-together songs that—

He froze as he looked over one song. It was easily the most worked-over, with dozens of corrections and erasures and marks of hard work. But as he read the words, he understood. And he knew what he had to do.

Lee wove down the hall, trying not to hit any of the residents with the guitar case. As he walked, he mentally reviewed the chords. He had practiced the song over the past week, stealing moments when he could. The tune was sloppy, and figuring out the song's melody had been tricky. But he was relatively confident he had reconstituted most of it. Hopefully, enough to work.

He turned the corner into B-104. Paula maintained her vigil. She jumped as Lee hurried in. She started to say something, but she stopped when her gaze fixed on the guitar. A question formed in her expression, but she didn't say anything as Lee moved to Mrs. White's side.

He set out Mr. White's notes and strummed through the song and then, after taking a deep breath, started singing. The rhymes were simple, the wording rough. Mr. White hadn't been a poet by any stretch of the imagination, but the song's lyrics were heartfelt, a tribute to building a life together. And the chorus?

*I'll build you a home, a place for us together.*

*I'll bring you home, just you and me.*

*So call me home from where I might wander*

*And I'll be at your side, Emily.*

Lee stumbled over the tune twice as he played. If Mr. White had written the tune on actual sheet music, maybe he could have done better. But based on what he saw, he suspected that Mr. White had figured all of this out as he went. That would have been his way.

It didn't matter. By the time Lee reached the second chorus, Mrs. White's eyes brightened. Instead of mumbling, she mouthed the lyrics with him. And as he wrapped up the song, she smiled at him, a pure expression of joy and recognition, free of confusion and clouds and doubt.

Paula put her hand on his shoulder and squeezed. "Thank you."

Lee returned Mrs. White's smile. He put his hand over Paula's and squeezed back. "My pleasure."

He knew he had more work ahead of him. The Whites' house needed help, probably more than he knew how to do. So did Paula and Matt and Mrs. White. And him too. He still needed a lot of answers about where to go next. But he'd figure it out. He could make a home for himself in the midst of the garbage, too. After all, if you love something, you figure out how to make it work.

# Notes on "The Home He Built"

ONCE AGAIN, I STARTED out round one absolutely stumped. This time around, I was told to write a drama about a brother-in-law and "self-taught." I had nothing. Absolutely nothing.

But then I remembered what happened when my wife had to move her parents into an assisted living facility. I remember how much work she and her brother had to do to clean up a house that their parents had been in for decades. And I remembered how much of that house had my father-in-law's touch. He had built these massive cabinets along one wall of the basement. He had constructed secret compartments where Christmas presents could be hidden.

Not only that, but at the time, I would visit members of my congregation in various nursing homes and care facilities. When I was training to be a pastor, he shared with me you could always tell if a care facility was good or not by what you smelled in the hallway.

All of those details came together. Toss in Lee's unrequited love for his sister-in-law, and I had the bones of a good story. The worst part was trying to write the words to the song.

Apparently, the judges thought so too. Unlike the previous year, I was able to move on to my next assignment.

# OPERATION OVERSHADOW



"BROTHER TOMAS, WITH ME."

Tripp froze at Bishop Balkus's quiet words. He fought to hide his nervousness. "Your Grace? I am behind on my duties and—"

Irritation flashed across Balkus's face. "Yes, cleaning offices is important and gives God and the motherland glory. But I have a more important job for you. Come."

The bishop injected steel into that last word, meaning Tripp didn't have a choice. He moved his janitor's cart out of the way and followed the bishop. As they walked, Tripp fought to keep calm. Why did the bishop have to interrupt him now, when he was on such a tight timeline? He fought the urge to touch the flash drive in his pocket. Had it somehow grown heavier in the last few seconds?

"Such a glorious day, yes? A day when Lithuania will become a shining city on a hill!" Balkus's voice sounded as if it echoed from stained glass.

Tripp forced himself to nod. That was one interpretation. Another was this: a Christian Nationalist cult led by the charismatic Mecys Gudelis had made troubling inroads into Lithuanian politics ever since Russia invaded Ukraine back in 2022. Against all odds, Gudelis was poised to be elected Lithuania's president in a predicted landslide.

"And on such a historic day, it is only proper that the world bears witness," Balkus continued.

Of course the world was paying attention. Gudelis believed God had called him to lead Lithuania on a grand crusade to unite the Baltic states under his banner and return them to Mother Russia's sphere of influence. If Gudelis was elected, all of Eastern Europe would be destabilized. The last thing this region needed was another war, and so yes, everyone was paying attention. The UN had sent in election observers. Reporters from all over the world had descended on Vilnius. And Langley had sent him. Finally in the field! He would prove the doubters wrong. His trainers. His superiors. His fellow agents. He could handle this. He'd show them. Tripp Larson would be a name whispered by those in power, the one who quietly saved Eastern Europe and, by extension, the world.

"And a foreigner wants to speak with you," Balkus said.

"M-me?" Tripp almost stumbled over his own feet. Why him? Had his cover been blown?

"Yes," Balkus said. "An American reporter wishes to interview a common man about Brother Gudelis's impending victory. And who is more common than Tomas Byla?"

The bishop laughed, and Tripp forced himself to join in. Balkus threw an arm around his shoulder and steered him into a crowded lobby. Dozens of reporters had set up camp here days ago, waiting for the election results. The bishop led him past reporters from Tokyo, Paris, and even Moscow, to a small cluster of Americans. Tripp looked them over. CNN. MSNBC. Even that new upstart, United American Prospect. Everyone waiting to hear the official results, delivered tonight once all the votes were tabulated and verified. The government wasn't taking any chances.

"Ms. Fredrickson, as requested, I present Tomas Byla, common man," Balkus said with a laugh.

The reporter turned around, and Tripp froze. Oh no.

She was gorgeous, more so than any woman had a right to be. But then, she always had been. Tripp remembered seeing her for the first time in the halls of Douglass High, how her laughter had quickened his heart, and just a glance from her was enough to melt his brain. The same blond hair. The same crystal-blue eyes. He knew her then as Michelle Park, the quintessential popular girl. Why was she here?

Michelle smiled at him, and he tensed. She'd blow his cover, and Operation Overshadow would be done. Five years of planning, two of deep cover work, all unraveled by a stupid quirk of—

She stuck out her hand. "So good to meet you, Mr. Byla. Do you mind answering a few questions?"

Wait, she didn't recognize him? He studied her face. No, it didn't appear that she did. For once, he was thankful for his bland features, his sandy blond hair, his brown eyes. Generic enough to pass for just about any European ethnicity. He smiled, clearing his throat, and prayed that his luck would hold.

"A pleasure to meet you, Ms. Fredrickson." He laid on the accent.

"Well, as Bishop Balkus said, I wanted to get the opinion of an ordinary person, and he suggested you. Why don't you tell me a little about yourself?" Michelle signaled her cameraman to start filming.

"Uh, well, my name is Tomas Byla. I'm from Kudrionys. You've heard of it?" he asked, injecting some hope into his voice.

She chuckled and shook her head.

"A small town north of here," Balkus interjected. "Very pleasant."

Tripp shot a sidelong glance at the bishop. Of course he would supervise the interview.

Michelle launched into clearly prepared questions: What did he think of Gudelis's grand vision for the Baltic states? What was his opinion of Gudelis's friendly attitude toward Moscow? Tripp answered them all, sticking to his backstory, parroting what Balkus would say. Glory to God. Glory to Lithuania. Glory to Gudelis. Everything would be sunshine and puppy farts once the election was over. And Michelle bought every lie. Tripp fought to keep from smiling. This is why he needed to be in the field. If he could trick her, he could handle anything.

"All right, last question. Mr. Byla, who did you vote for?" she asked.

He chuckled. "Gudelis, of course."

"Well, thank you so much, and—"

One of the other reporters tripped over their own cables and slammed into Michelle. She pitched forward. Tripp caught her. She looked into his eyes, and his mouth went dry. She smelled of lilacs, and her hands on his arms were gentle, almost a caress. She took a few stuttering breaths, looking absolutely shocked. Helpless.

So beautiful.

"Are you all right?" he whispered.

She nodded. "Thanks to you."

He steadied her, and she smoothed her clothes. The man who tripped apologized to her, which she accepted graciously. Then she offered a few more words to the camera before wrapping up the interview.

"Well, thank you, Mr. Byla," she said once the camera was off.

"Please call me Tomas."

"Only if you'll call me Michelle."

"I'd rather call you for drinks," he said. "Maybe tonight?"

She stared at him, her eyes wide. Of course, he couldn't follow through. He'd leave Vilnius that evening, but if she took the bait, how much sweeter would his victory be? A gift to his teenage self, the one Michelle had so studiously ignored.

"We'll see." She slipped him her card. "If you'll excuse me."

He smiled and pocketed it next to the flash drive, all the while wanting to crow at her gullibility. She turned back to the other reporters.

Balkus cleared his throat. "Brother Tomas, your duties?"

Tripp nodded and made his way back to his cart. By his estimation, he still had plenty of time, but he couldn't dawdle.

Once he retrieved his cart, he pushed it down the hall to a nearby office, one usually occupied by some bureaucratic number cruncher. Thankfully, he followed a strict routine. For the next ten minutes, he'd be in the nearest bathroom, dealing with the aftereffects of cheap coffee. More than enough time.

Producing a set of keys, Tripp opened the door and slipped inside. Sure enough, it was empty. But it wouldn't stay that way for long. He hustled to the desk and double-checked. Yes, the computer was still logged on and connected to the government's mainframe. He smirked. *Thank you, lazy government officials.*

Tripp pulled the thumb drive from his pocket and slipped it into an available USB port. A few mouse clicks and the virus slipped into the government's network. Tripp had no idea how the stupid thing worked, but his superiors had assured him of the basics: once loose in the network, it would find the official vote tallies and corrupt them, making it look like Gudelis received far fewer votes than anyone expected. Oh, there would be outcries, to be sure. The Russians would accuse the West of meddling. Conspiracy theorists would spin their wild tales of an unexpected undercount. But with so many UN observers and watchdogs in place? Gudelis's grand vision for the future would be derailed, and it was all thanks to Special Agent Tripp Larson.

Gudelis won? *How the hell did that happen?*

After planting the virus, Tripp had followed his exit plan: he left by train from Vilnius to Suwalki in Poland. There he holed up in a cheap motel. He had gotten some krupnik from a shop near the train station and had planned to toast his success throughout the night. But then, when he turned on the TV, he saw the impossible news. The BBC, CNN, Al Jazeera, even Rossiya 1 was reporting the same bewildering story: in a historic landslide, Mecys Gudelis had been elected as Lithuania's newest president.

How was this possible? What had gone wrong?

There was a knock at the door. Tripp growled and went over. Whoever dared to bother him would regret it!

He opened the door and froze.

Michelle Fredrickson smirked at him. "I thought we were going to go for drinks, lover."

He gaped at her as she brushed past him into the room.

She looked around, clucking her tongue. "You'd think Langley would spring for better accommodations than this. But then, they did kinda half-ass this whole operation from the get-go."

She tossed him something. He caught it out of the air and stared dumbly at the thumb drive, the one he had tossed out the window of the train as they crossed the Polish border.

"That's the real one, by the way," she said.

He looked up at her, then replayed the interview in his mind. Her stumble into him. Clinging to his arm as she righted herself...

"You swapped them," he whispered.

"Basic pickpocketing. I thought for sure you'd notice. Glad you didn't."

He sat down hard on the bed, watching as she picked up the bottle of krupnik. She examined the label, then shrugged and poured two glasses. She handed one to him.

"Might as well enjoy it while you can. I suspect you're going to be feeling some heat from Washington pretty soon."

That was putting it mildly. He swallowed the honeyed liquor, heat spreading through his chest. There were so many questions, but only one rose to the surface: "Why?"

"Big picture? The DGSE doesn't agree with the CIA's opinion on what kind of leader Gudelis will be. Well, especially since he technically works for us."

Tripp stared at her, aghast. She worked for French intelligence? Gudelis was their asset? Since when?

"Smaller picture? When I heard you were going into the field, how could I pass up an opportunity to see a hometown friend?" She slammed her drink and set the empty glass on the counter. "Now, if you'll excuse me, I have a debriefing to get to. Don't worry. I'm sure Langley will have bigger fish to fry by the time all this blows over. But hey, if worse comes to worst, call me. I'm sure the DGSE could find a job for you somewhere. Ta ta."

With that, she breezed out of the room, leaving Tripp to stew in what he had just heard. Was it really possible that Gudelis worked for the French? Did Michelle? Or was this just disinformation to muddy the waters?

He finally sighed and finished his drink. Glory to God. Glory to Lithuania. Glory to Gudelis. And nothing left for him.

# Notes on "Operation Overshadow"

ROUND TWO THAT YEAR was interesting. I had to write a spy story about an undercount and an interviewee. What was I supposed to do with that?

Well, people were discussing the rise of Christian Nationalism at the time, and Russia had just invaded Ukraine. I decided to pull from current events and see what I could come up with. I also pulled from a book series about how to be a spy that I read when I was a kid.

Once again, I leaned into my love of twists. Maybe that was my downfall. Once again, my contest journey ended here.

# HER PLACE IN THE PAGES

Celestine tried to remind herself that she belonged in the ballroom. She had been invited to Princess Erdissa's Nameday Banquet. This was her chance to find her place in court. But as she watched the guests, she realized she didn't really fit.

The only other person as detached from the revelry as Celestine was the princess's attendant, Lady Alyndra. Celestine's gaze kept drifting in her direction. She didn't know why. Not because of Alyndra's beauty. Most would consider her plain. Nor her dress. She wore a shockingly simple dress. So why couldn't Celestine stop staring at her?

"Trying to decipher Alyndra, are we?"

The whispered question caused Celestine to jump, almost dropping her wine. She turned, realizing Lady Starla and her pack of sycophants had surrounded her. Celestine dipped into a curtsy since Starla's family outranked hers. Starla waited until Celestine finished, haughty approval shining in her eyes. A thrill of hope shot through Celestine. If she could impress her, maybe this would all work out.

"Not at all," Celestine said. "But she is a puzzle, isn't she? She hasn't danced with anyone, and she hasn't eaten anything either. She seems perfectly content to stare at—"

Starla's friends giggled. Celestine quickly clamped her mouth shut. Her words had undermined her denial.

Starla studied her face. "You're supposed to be part of the princess's watch tonight, yes?"

Celestine nodded. Father had somehow called in enough favors to get her that honor. She and a dozen other young women would "patrol" the palace while Princess Erdissa slept. There was no way Celestine deserved the position, but it was all part of the game. It would allow her to mingle with other nobles and hopefully make the right friendships.

"Then this is perfect. I would ask you to do me a service."

Even better! According to tradition, other nobles could ask those chosen to patrol to do them favors. Usually, it involved playing harmless pranks. Another opportunity? Only if she took it. "Of course, Lady Starla. What is your pleasure?"

Starla offered a predatory smile. "I've learned that Alyndra keeps a diary. She's most secretive about it. So tonight, I want you to find the diary and bring it to me."

Celestine's blood ran cold. A simple enough request, but it still caused her heart to stutter. What would happen if she got caught?

She glanced over her shoulder to where Alyndra watched the guests, her gaze roving from person to person. For a moment, their eyes met. Alyndra held hers, and Celestine noticed for the first time how blue the other woman's were. So crystal clear, like a summer's day, even from across the room.

"I'll do it," Celestine whispered.

Sharla laughed and clapped her hands. "Excellent! And once you do, I promise that I'll make sure you're invited to all the right parties. Trust me, Celestine. Your life will truly begin."

Celestine tried to smile. Exactly what Father wanted. Exactly what she needed. So why was her stomach fluttering at the mere thought of entering Alyndra's room?

As it turned out, the others chosen to stand watch had no intention of actually patrolling. Instead, they had hidden themselves in Erdissa's room to drink and gossip. Celestine tried to join in, but the other girls treated her like a nuisance. As they continued to drink and gossip, Celestine realized she'd make no friends there. She really only had one choice.

Holding her breath, Celestine slipped out of the princess's quarters. She tried not to make a sound, but then, the princess and her overnight guests were making such a ruckus she doubted they'd notice her absence.

Darkness had transformed the palace. When she first arrived before the banquet, Celestine had been overwhelmed by the beauty and grandeur. And why not? Magnificent works of art filled every nook and cranny, and even the walls and floors were masterpieces of patterns worked into the marble.

But in the night, the palace took on a sinister air. The shadows pulsed to a languid rhythm, encroaching and then retreating as Celestine slunk through the halls. While she could hear the distant footsteps of guards, an oppressive quiet chased her.

Then she passed a stained-glass window that towered over her, and she froze. She had seen this earlier that day. It depicted King Berlys, Erdissa's father, fighting the Irdiki barbarians. Her tutors had told her the story of that military campaign. But the images had changed. The king appeared overwhelmed, cowering from his oncoming foes. And the enemies he faced were no longer Irdiki, but a ravenous horde of monstrosities with glowing eyes, sharp fangs, and even longer claws. The people who fought at the king's side were no longer knights and foot soldiers but strangely clad individuals with curved weapons. A chill swept through Celestine. A trick of the light. It had to be.

She hurried on until she came to Lady Alyndra's door. Taking a deep breath, Celestine rapped a knuckle against the door. "Lady Alyndra? Are you awake?"

She braced herself, then panicked as she realized she hadn't come up with a reason to knock on Alyndra's door in the middle of the night. What excuse could she possibly have? The princess needed her? No, Erdissa likely had a way of summoning Alyndra. There was an emergency that required Alyndra's attention? But what could that possibly be?

She had been intrigued by the mysterious woman at the party, and her curiosity had finally gotten the better of her?

Celestine's cheeks heated at the thought. She knocked again and leaned in to hear any response. Only silence. She tested the door and found it unlocked. With another shuddering breath, she slipped inside.

Alyndra's room turned out to be much like the woman herself: austere and somewhat cold. In spite of the large room, the only furnishings were a gigantic bed, a simple vanity, a wardrobe, and a bare desk. There was nothing frivolous or decorative. In some ways, that was good; it would make her search easier. But at the same time, she was disappointed. This had been a chance to learn more about Alyndra and there was very little to see.

She checked the desk first, but a quick inspection revealed nothing. No papers, quills, ink, or anything. The vanity had simple cosmetics and nothing else. Celestine steered clear of the bed and opened the wardrobe. Alyndra didn't have much in there either, just simple dresses and outfits. But then Celestine spotted her quarry: a leather-bound book at the bottom of the wardrobe.

Celestine quickly snatched it up and headed for the door. Success! She imagined Starla's grateful look, the new friendships that would blossom from this one act. Father would be so pleased. Giving this to Starla would ensure Celestine's rise in the court.

But then she hesitated. What would Starla actually do with the diary? Probably spread the contents through rumors and gossip. Was Celestine okay with that possibility? She knew she should be. A minor price to pay for her family's good. But would Alyndra's life be ruined? Or would the princess's? Alyndra was with Erdissa constantly and probably recorded many salacious details that could humiliate the princess if revealed. What scandals lurked in the diary's pages? What damage could Starla wreak with the diary's contents?

She glanced at the book and felt an overwhelming desire to look for herself, if only to reassure herself. If there were anything scandalous, she'd put it back. Besides, what could it hurt, one little peek?

Celestine swallowed a nervous giggle and cracked open the book to a blank page.

She blinked, surprised. So she flipped to another page, only to find that one was blank as well. She jumped to another spot. More empty pages. She rifled through the entire diary and found absolutely nothing. No words. No scribbles. Nothing at all.

As she flipped through the diary again, she spotted something. Not writing, but a strange shimmering along one page's edge, a coruscating glimmer. At first, she thought it was a trick of the eye, maybe from the lingering rush of being in Alyndra's room. But when Celestine turned back to the page, she saw it again, more clearly. Light bled down the page, flowing toward the spine and revealing strange symbols. Soon the page was covered in glyphs, a soft glow of reds and greens and blues undulating over the surface. She checked the rest of the diary. The pages that had been blank just a few moments before were now filled with symbols, glowing in the near darkness.

Celestine bit her lower lip. She felt as though she should shove the diary back into its hiding place and flee. But there was something that drew her eyes to the patterns. The glow seemed to fill her chest with a strange warmth. Without thinking, she touched one of the symbols.

*she stood on a heat-blasted plain, the trees and bushes blackened and gnarled. she tightened the grip on her sword and set herself, staring down the shadows that charged across the cracked dirt*

She nearly dropped the book, the room snapping back into focus. Her heart slammed in her chest, but she could swear she could still feel the heat from wherever that had been. What was that?

The symbol she had touched pulsed for a few heartbeats, then returned to normal. So Celestine gritted her teeth and touched another.

*the water only came up to her knees, but she could feel the tendrils worming around her ankles. She would have to hurry before they dragged her under, but her liege was in danger and she*

Celestine snatched her finger away. Then she pressed it against another symbol.

*the brilliant night sky stretched far overhead, and for just a moment, she felt true peace and comfort in*

Another.

*knife and claws clashing together, sending a shower of sparks into*

Another.

*gentle brush of skin against her lips as she*

Another!

*searing pain as her shoulder*

Something ripped the book from her hands. Celestine jumped, only to find herself face-to-face with Alyndra. She hadn't realized how short the other woman was. She barely came up to Celestine's chin. And yet, with the fury blazing in her eyes, Alyndra seemed to tower over her.

"What do you think you are doing?" Alyndra demanded.

Celestine's mouth went dry. Her mind spun, and she felt as if she had been wrenched out of a dream.

"I asked you a question!" Alyndra said.

Before Celestine could reply, a low moan rumbled through the floor. Celestine felt it in her feet, and her mind twisted at the sound. It was wrong. Broken.

Alyndra growled. "Of all the rotten timing."

Then Alyndra balled her hands into fists. When she did, the shadows in the room rushed to her hands, twisting and knitting together to form two long swords with curved blades. Alyndra looked at Celestine and her eyes glowed a hazy red.

"Stay here." Her voice had taken on an odd warble. "I'll deal with you shortly."

With that, Alyndra dashed out of the door.

Celestine stood in the darkness, unable to move, barely able to breathe. The moaning continued, only to suddenly pitch louder and higher into an ear-rending shriek. And then silence. That was worse than the noise.

Then the door popped open and Alyndra staggered in. Her hair was disheveled and her clothing had been torn. She swiped blood away from her mouth.

"Are...are you okay?" Celestine whispered.

Alyndra grunted. "Been better. Be a lot better if you don't waste my time. What are you doing here?"

The story spilled out of Celestine without any more prompting. Alyndra listened to her rambling story, her only reaction an arched eyebrow as she described what she saw when she touched the diary. When Celestine finished her tale, Alyndra swore under her breath.

"This 'Starla' dares you to invade my privacy, and you just do it?"

Excuses popped into her head: her need to forge friendships for her family's benefit, Starla's request, her own curiosity. But those thoughts vanished beneath Alyndra's withering glare. "I-I'm sorry."

Alyndra cursed again. "I should've been more careful. Prying maids always cause us trouble." She gave Celestine a curious look. "But you could see what was inside? And you saw the truth in the window?"

Celestine nodded.

"Interesting. We haven't found someone with that capability in a generation."

What did that mean? But a different question clawed its way out of her mouth. "Who are you?"

Alyndra laughed, a mirthless bark. "That could take a while to explain. Let's just say that my sisters and I have been protecting the royal family for the past six hundred years."

"Why?"

"Ancient prophecy. A long-awaited deliverer from their line. The fate of humanity hanging in the balance." She said it with a wave, as if this was simple as anything.

"Really?" Celestine thought of the half-drunk girl she had left surrounded by other revelers. That didn't seem likely.

"That's what our superiors tell us," Alyndra said with a shrug. "And the way the enemy keeps attacking them, they seem to believe it as well. So here we are."

Celestine digested that. Then she met Alyndra's hard glare. "So, now what?"

Alyndra's brow furrowed, and she studied Celestine's face, her gaze then sweeping down to her feet. Celestine resisted the urge to squirm under the intense scrutiny.

"That's a good question. I see this ending two different ways: you could take the book to this Starla and give it to her. You might get the recognition you're hoping for, although she probably will only see blank pages, so who knows if she'll believe it's my diary."

That was true. If Starla only had an empty book, she might think Celestine was trying to trick her. There was no way that any of this would work.

"Or…"

Celestine's ears perked up.

Alyndra studied her, her face grim. "You have the sight. You could join our order."

Celestine started to speak, but Alyndra held up a finger.

"It's not a simple path. It could easily break you. And what we do must remain hidden from everyone. But if you're willing, I can train you."

Celestine's breath caught in her throat. Working with Alyndra, entering this new world, this new adventure. Finding a place for herself, even if it might be difficult or dangerous. But that didn't worry her.

She nodded. "When do we begin?"

Alyndra smiled, and the genuine warmth in the expression caused Celestine's heart to stutter. This may not be what Father had intended, but Celestine knew in that moment she had truly found her place.

# Notes on "Her Place in the Pages"

With the first round of 2023, I was told to write a fantasy about a diary and a lady-in-waiting. I felt pretty confident about this one. Celestine, Alyndra, the fight scene. It all came together so quickly, and I felt so very confident. I thought for sure I'd make it to the next round.

*Womp womp.*

Actually, I think I understand why they decided that way now. As I prepared this story for this anthology, I discovered an embarrassing number of spelling and grammatical errors. Apparently, I didn't proofread enough.

Oh, well. On to the next year, I guess.

# Necessary Sacrifices

It was only Tuesday morning. Yet Simon felt as if he was carrying the stress of a full week already. When Tanya stuck her head into his office, his mounting headache twisted into a painful knot.

"What?"

"W-we've got another complaint from Nora," Tanya said.

Simon groaned. Why couldn't it be past noon so he could take a slug from the vodka he had stashed in his drawer? Bad enough that everyone was doing overtime. Bad enough they had to be wary of competitors and the press trying to suss out what they were up to. Now this?

"Let me guess. Adrienne messed with the 'babies.'"

Tanya offered him a sympathetic smile.

Simon ground his teeth. "Fine."

He struggled to keep his frustration hidden as he entered "the Playground." Simon hated the layout: random desks strewn through the space, punctuated by three foosball tables, a cereal bar, and an enormous pile of beanbags. But Dermot Garcia, Nostra's wunderkind founder, insisted this loosey-goosey atmosphere resulted in "synergistic workflow leading to explosive innovation." Garcia seemed to barely understand the corporate babble he spewed, but Simon couldn't argue with the results. Nostra had churned out innovations every other quarter, the greatest of which was going to be their next, an operating system for

PCs nicknamed "Firelord." Since Garcia signed the checks, Simon had to make it work. Even if—

"Mr. Jones!" Nora stormed through the Playground.

Simon braced himself. "I'm looking into it, but I'm willing to bet—"

"I don't care!" Nora stomped her foot. "Adrienne did it! You need to do something!"

Oh, he'd love to do something to both of them, but he couldn't. Nora was an incredible accountant, and in the short time she had worked here, she had found close to two dozen different ways to streamline his department's budget. That made his superiors happy, which meant he had to keep her happy, which was nearly impossible. Especially when it came to her "babies."

When Nora first started, she brought in eleven porcelain dolls, each one three feet tall and wearing ratty, old-fashioned clothing. She had propped them up around the perimeter of her workstation. She claimed she had inherited them from her grandmother. Technically, Nostra permitted that kind of grandiose personalization, but Nora's collection of her "babies" had quickly caused friction with her coworkers. After Nora's venomous glares and sharp comments, most of the Playground's denizens learned to leave the dolls alone.

Except for Adrienne. She was one of the best programmers in the company, brought in to help finish Firelord. That meant Simon had to keep her mollified too. As much as he'd like to be rid of both of them, he couldn't, so he found himself refereeing this bizarre feud more than he should have.

"Show me," Simon said.

Nora led him over to her desk. Even as they approached, Simon could see the problem. Nora usually had her dolls lined up in height order, but two of them had obviously changed places. Not only that, they now wore booty shorts and crop tops. He had no idea how Adrienne kept pulling these pranks without being spotted.

"Do you see?" Nora stabbed a finger at the dolls. "Persimmon and Buttercup aren't in their spots. And I don't know where their dresses went!"

Simon turned to Adrienne, who was doing her best to pretend she was engrossed in whatever was happening on her laptop, but he could tell she was watching the events unfold with a sly smile. He beckoned for her.

She bounced over, offering him a bright smile. "What's up, Simon?"

He waved toward the dolls.

Adrienne looked them over, an exaggeratedly worried expression on her face. "Did something happen to Messywinkle and Cummerbund? Nora, I'm so sorry. I'm sure this must be absolutely devastating to you!"

"You did this!" Nora's face had turned nearly purple in an instant. "This morning, while I was upstairs at the financial planning meeting."

"Not possible. I was over at Snitsky's desk, running sims on the Firelord code. You can ask him."

Simon would, knowing full well that Snitsky would say whatever Adrienne wanted him to. He obviously had a crush on Adrienne.

"You can always check the security footage." Adrienne jerked a thumb toward a nearby camera.

That would be worthless as well, even though security at Nostra was the tightest it'd ever been. Because Firelord would be such a game changer, Garcia had ordered a complete lockdown. More cameras, bag checks going in and out, no personal laptops or hard drives allowed in, no company tech allowed out. And yet Adrienne somehow knew how to avoid observation when she pulled these pranks.

"I demand you discipline her, Mr. Jones!" Nora said.

Simon screwed his eyes shut. He knew how this would go. He'd chide Adrienne for picking on Nora. Adrienne would promise to be good. Nora would eventually drop it. And then he'd have peace for a week or two before Adrienne got bored and did it all over again.

As he thought through what he could say, his gaze hitched on a middle-aged man perched on the arm of a couch in the conversation pit, chatting with a few of the Playground's residents. For a split second, he didn't recognize him. But just as the question formed in his mouth, he remembered: Mike Simpson, a PI who was trying to dig up dirt on Erik Blaze, one of Nostra's former employees who was caught in a nasty divorce. He had been poking around the Playground for the past few days, gathering stories. As near as Simon could tell, he hadn't found much and, thankfully, he was staying out of the way. But it was one more annoyance to add to the stack of so many others.

"Look, I'm going to make this simple." He jabbed a finger at Adrienne. "Just stay out of her stuff." As Adrienne objected, he whirled on Nora. "Maybe take the dolls home? They really don't belong here."

Nora bristled. "If I can't have them here, then you need to tell Logan that he can't have his action figures or tell Samantha she can't keep those photos!"

Simon gaped at her. "Those are of her kids!"

"And these are mine!" Nora's voice went shrill.

Simon chewed back a groan. "Just leave each other alone, okay?"

Adrienne held up her hands in surrender. "Hey, boss, no worries. I'll just be over here in the doll-free zone."

Nora spluttered, but then she spun and stormed back to her desk. Some tension drained from Simon's body, but not all of it. With this fire out, he might get some actual work done.

As he made his way back to his office, he spotted Tanya waiting by the door, a frantic look on her face. She looked scared to death. She started to say something, but then motioned for him to go into his office. He sighed. What now?

He stopped short at the sight of the large man in a three-piece suit standing next to his desk. He looked as if he could rip Simon in half.

"Simon Jones?" The man's voice was little more than a growl.

Simon swallowed hard. "Th-that's me, yes."

The man reached into his jacket pocket and, for a split second, Simon worried he would pull a gun. Instead, he pulled out a leather wallet and flashed a badge at him.

"Charlie Weathers, FBI." Weathers reached into his jacket again and pulled out a picture, handing it to Simon. "You know this guy?"

Simon blinked. "Yeah, that's Mike Simpson. He's an investigator doing work on a divorce. One of our former employees supposedly had an affair. Something about how that would invalidate his prenup or something."

Weathers snorted. "Is that what he said?"

"That's not true?"

The big man shook his head. "His name's not Mike Simpson. His real name's Everett Olson. He's a con man who's been traveling up and down the East Coast looking for victims. He impersonates private investigators and trawls for information he can use in a scam."

Cold swept through Simon. A con artist? Here? Was he after Firelord? That would be a disaster.

Weathers held up his hands in a calming gesture. "Relax, Mr. Jones. Olson doesn't target corporations. He's probably after that employee you mentioned. You seen Olson recently?"

Simon frowned. How had Weathers missed him when he came onto the floor? He pointed toward the Playground. "Well, yeah, right out there, and—"

Weathers practically shoved Simon out of the way. Simon hurried after him, emerging in time to hear the FBI agent bellow Olson's name. The other man bolted from his perch, leading Weathers on a chase through the Playground. Weathers shouted for Olson to stop, but the conman wasn't going to. Simpson—or Olson, or whoever—rounded the corner by Adrienne's desk, heading for the nearest stairwell...

Only Adrienne stuck out her foot and tripped him. He scrambled, trying to regain his footing, but he stumbled forward, his arms pinwheeling...

And as he caromed past Nora's desk, his flailing arm smacked one doll off her perch. The porcelain doll flew up in the air, only to hit the floor with a loud crash, shattering on impact.

The entire Playground went silent, but then that was pierced by a high-pitched shriek as Nora came out of her desk to scoop up the pieces of her doll.

Simon groaned and closed his eyes as his headache flared. He would never hear the end of this.

A conman smashing Nora's doll turned out to be a blessing in disguise. At least, that's the way Simon saw things by the end of the day.

Once Agent Weathers manhandled Olson out of the Playground, Simon spent close to three hours consoling Nora over her "loss." She wasn't having it. It didn't help that Weathers had praised Adrienne for her help. In between crying jags, she accused Adrienne of somehow orchestrating the entire thing. When he tried to point out to her that that was ridiculous, she had turned her venom on him, claiming he was in on it as well. He tried to deny it, but that only prompted her to quit on the spot. She packed up all of her remaining dolls and personal effects and, screaming insults at everyone, stormed out of the building. Simon was so glad to see her go, he quietly told security to just let her leave.

Adrienne offered him a sympathetic smile once the shrieking harpy had left the Playground. But everyone got back to work, focusing on Firelord's release. And by the end of the day, much of the tension Simon had carried with him melted away. Sure, his superiors would squawk, but he could spin this as being good for morale, his especially. Maybe it hadn't been such a bad day after all.

She spotted her contact the moment she stepped into Hooligan's. She snorted. Idiot. She had picked this dive for their rendezvous because the patrons valued their anonymity. And yet there he was, dressed like a corporate drone in a shirt and tie, in stark contrast to everyone else. He might as well have worn a neon sign. She sauntered through the bar, ignoring the looks that the men she passed gave her.

Her contact looked up as she slid into the booth. "You have it?"

She smiled and set her purse on the table. "Ten hard drives, filled with data on Firelord. Proprietary code, beta-testing feedback, maintenance projections. More than enough for your team to leapfrog over them and beat them to market first."

He nodded, a bead of sweat appearing on his forehead. "How'd you get this past security?"

She smiled sweetly. "Honey, don't ask stupid questions you don't want to know the answer to."

He flinched, but then fumbled at the purse's zipper. His head jerked up, and he glared at her.

"Why is this locked?" he demanded.

"I don't see my fee," she countered.

He grunted, then pulled out a briefcase and slid it across the table. She peeked inside. She wouldn't count the money in front of him. Looked like all two million was there.

She shot him a smile and produced the key. "Pleasure doing business with you."

Gripping the briefcase's handle, she calmly walked out of the bar and crossed the street to the waiting car. She didn't breathe again until she was in the backseat and they pulled away from the curb.

Benny whirled around from the passenger seat. She winced when she saw the bruise on his cheek. He must have hit the floor too hard when Sally tripped him. Or maybe Hank hit him while pretending to arrest him. He sometimes got a little rough.

"We got the cash?" he asked.

She raised the briefcase. "Like you have to ask. Two million, as promised."

Hank said nothing from the driver's seat, remaining focused on the road. She offered him an enticing smile. They'd have their own celebration later. Maybe she'd make him wear the suit and pretend he was still FBI, spice things up a little.

"What about Sally?" Benny asked. "Shouldn't she have quit too?"

She shook her head. "Too obvious. If both of us quit at the same time, Nostra would tumble to who stole the data. No, Sally will keep working there, but in a few weeks, she'll accuse Snitsky of ogling her one too many times and quit. Relax, Benny. Everything went exactly as I planned."

Benny grumbled something under his breath, but turned around. She leaned into the seat, breathing out a long breath, thankful that her headache unwound.

When she was hired to steal Nostra's Firelord, she knew she couldn't do it alone. Working with Hank had been a given. But she had needed Sally's nimble hacking to get the goods. Benny, as annoying as he was, gave her the perfect cover to smuggle out the hard drives in the remaining dolls. She didn't enjoy splitting their finder's fee, but she had to.

She pulled the face of the broken doll out of her pocket. Its edges were sharp against her fingers, and she felt a pang of remorse. When Grandma Arlene gave her that collection, she had made her promise to take care of them. And she had. She loved those dolls. Breaking one felt like a worse crime than any of the others they had committed.

She pushed aside her remorse. Sometimes you had to break a few faces to get ahead in life. Benny's. The doll's. Necessary sacrifices. And so she rolled down the window of the car and tossed the porcelain remnants onto the street and leaned back with a contented sigh as the last vestiges of the headache disappeared into the deepening night.

# Notes on "Necessary Sacrifices"

Another year, another #ShortStoryChallenge, and my first round heat in 2024 was to write a crime caper about trade secrets and a doll collector. I love a good, complicated heist story. You know, like the TV show *Leverage* or the movie *Ocean's Eleven*. But how do you tell one in 2,000 words? I recall going over the word limit multiple times while drafting this story. The rewriting process was brutal, cutting little details and streamlining the heist details until I finally got it under the limit.

The judges seemed to like the result. I went on to the next round with...

# BURYING THE DEMON

My job's usually simple. Go where I'm told, deal with drivers, tow the offending vehicle to a service station. Clock in, clock out.

Never thought I'd get to bury my demon.

I had already worked eight hours that Saturday, but I stayed on for extra because, first, it's overtime. Second, Bob had been short-handed for three months. And third, it's not like anyone would miss me at home. Then I got the call at two in the morning: car in the ditch out on County 125 near 307th. With a glance at Angie's picture taped to the dash, I pulled onto Fremont's darkened streets. I rolled past the shadowy houses, the closed-down businesses, allowing a smile to tickle my lips. I preferred my hometown like this. No one giving me those pitying looks or whispering about my history.

Buildings gave way to fields. Fog enveloped me, reducing the world to a circle around my truck. I eventually saw the car's headlights stabbing into the air like searchlights. I flipped on my ambers and pulled over. The cold air slithered across my skin. A kid in his mid-twenties stood at the side of the road, staring vacantly at the car.

"You okay?" I called.

He turned to me, and my breath caught in my throat.

He was older than the last time I had seen him. His hair hung to his shoulders, brown instead of the bleached blond it had been during the trial. But I recognized the shape of his eyes, his narrow face.

It was him. Michael Manchester. Angie's killer.

He stepped toward me, and his foot slipped on the gravel. He steadied himself, laughing, and pushed the hair out of his eyes. "Took my eyes off the road for a second and next thing I knew…"

I nodded stiffly, my body colder than it had any reason to be. That lazy smile, the same one he wore when the judge tossed the case. I could still hear echoes of the prosecutor's apologies as Michael had turned to face Tammy and me, smirking because he'd walk out of the courtroom free.

As he approached me, the musty scent of beer washed over me. He reeked of it.

"You been drinkin'?"

"Nah, man. My cousins and I were at a party and… this guy dumped a bottle on my shirt." He held out the fabric, but it looked dry to me. "No way I'd drive if I'd had anything to drink."

My jaw clenched at the obvious lie, the same one he had told the deputies when they arrested him. *I would never drink and drive.* Except he had. We all knew it, even though that judge had dismissed the case with prejudice.

"So, can you help me?" he asked.

Why didn't he recognize me? Maybe I had changed too much. Tammy said I had aged twenty years during the trial. It was part of the reason she left me. I had dropped weight since then, too. Most people said I was a shadow of the man I had been. And they were right. This demon had consumed so much of me.

I nodded stiffly and headed for the ditch, my mind whirling through possibilities. I should call this in. Sheriff Okuda would love to get reacquainted with Michael. But what was the point? Michael's parents would just send in their high-powered lawyers again.

"You from around here?" I asked.

"Not anymore."

I remembered the day I heard that Michael and his family had skipped town. Local paper said they "wanted to leave the unfortunate incident behind them." As if they could just dump Michael's guilt on the side of the road like so much garbage.

"I'm visiting my cousins, remember?"

"Right. So where are they?"

He looked down at the road. "They, uh… they didn't want to leave."

Interesting. I clambered down to look over the car. The wheels had dug into the mud, deep enough that the car couldn't have worked itself free. Wouldn't be a problem for my truck, though.

"Can you help me or not?" Michael's voice had an edge to it.

"You in a hurry?" I asked.

"Kind of." He rubbed the back of his neck. "I never should have come back here."

No, he shouldn't have. But he had. Life had finally given me what I truly needed. In that moment, I knew what I had to do.

I cleared my throat. "This won't take more than a minute. Hang on, let me go get some gear and I'll take care of you."

He smiled at me, and my stomach curdled. I forced myself to mirror the expression. Then I went back to the truck. I climbed into the cab and took several deep breaths, calming myself. How often had I prayed for a chance like this? I had begged God to do what the courts hadn't, and yet, for the past eight years, Michael had skated through life, doing all the things Angie never would. Like going off to college. Going to parties. Living.

Well, that was all going to end now. I grabbed the two things I needed and headed back to the ditch.

As I approached, Michael looked at me, a question forming on his face. I didn't allow him to speak. Instead, I held up the picture of Angie I had always had taped to my dashboard. Her sophomore school picture, the last one she'd ever been able to take. His gaze flicked to it, then back to my face. But then he looked back at the photo. His face went ashen, and he stumbled back a step.

"Mr. Lewis? But I thought... they said you and Mrs. Lewis had moved out of town!"

I snarled. Yes, Tammy and her new husband had left town two years earlier, wanting to get a fresh start in California. And so many people had encouraged me to do something similar. But how could I when my entire world was buried in Candlewood Cemetery?

Before he could say another word, I pulled the Sig out of my pocket and leveled it at him. He froze, his hands up. I bared my teeth at him, a vicious smile. Once I pulled the trigger, I would stuff his body in the trunk of his car and tow it to Leo's Service Station. On my way home, I'd throw the gun into the hole they'd dug for the high school's new addition. They were going to pour the cement first thing in the morning. Yeah, they'd come talk to me, but I'd say I couldn't find Michael and just towed his car. I had no idea what had happened to him. Sheriff Okuda would believe me.

Michael sank to his knees, his chest heaving. He held out his hands as if he could catch the bullet or block it. But then his shoulders slumped.

"Just... just go ahead," he whispered.

I frowned. What was this nonsense?

He looked up at me. "You'd be doing me a favor. I haven't had a good night's sleep for the last seven years, man. Every time I close my eyes, I see...her. I hear the screech of my tires. The thump. All of it. Over and over."

"Then why didn't you plead guilty?" My voice was thick with anger.

"I wanted to! My dad wouldn't let me. He said throwing away my life wouldn't bring Angie back. So I figured the jury would do it for me. Only then, the mistrial? What was I supposed to do?"

My hand holding the gun trembled. "Why are you even here?"

He sighed. "I thought maybe I could find some peace, y'know? But my cousins took me to that party."

"Where you were drinking!" I jabbed the gun at him.

"No! I haven't touched a drop since that night, I swear! But someone recognized who I was, and they dumped their beer on me. I knew everyone else would figure it out, so I had to get out of there." He met my gaze. "And now here you are. It's pretty clear the universe won't let me escape anymore. So go ahead."

He dropped his head. I glared at him, but the gun had become so heavy. I tried to muster the anger I needed to hold it steady, to pull the trigger, but as I stared at Michael, I didn't see a killer. I saw him for what he was: tired. Broken. Carrying the weight of what he had done.

Just like me.

With a grunt, I sat down across from him. He looked up, startled. We stared at each other for what felt like years.

"You know, I bought this during your trial." I held up the gun. "When they started talking about a possible mistrial. I had this idea I would bring it with me to the courthouse if things went...well, the way they did."

His eyes locked onto the weapon. "Why didn't you?"

I sighed heavily. "Tammy found out. She hid it. I didn't find it until after the divorce."

The silence hung heavy between us, thick as the fog.

"I know it won't change anything, but I am sorry," he said. "I know I wrecked your life. If it's any consolation, I wrecked mine too."

It wasn't. But I said, "Tell me."

He looked just as surprised as I felt. He didn't say anything, not at first. Probably didn't want to provoke me. So I tucked the gun away and asked him some gentle questions, and soon it all spilled out. His constant nightmares. Leaving Fremont to "start fresh," as his dad put it. Nearly failing out of his new high school. Dropping out of college. Bouncing from job to job, always chased by the demon of what he'd done. He didn't lie to me once. I could hear the truth woven into his words, see it painted over his face. This wasn't a ploy or a scheme for my sympathy. I could see the burden pressing down on him, nearly crushing him.

As he shared, I did too. The pitying looks from my neighbors. Tammy's demands that I "get over it." Losing my job at the bank. The divorce. The tiny apartment. The more we talked, the more the certainty grew. Michael and I weren't that much different. We were both haunted by the same demon. And we both needed it gone.

Finally, the first streaks of dawn cut through the fog. I blinked at the bright light and chuckled. Bob would grouse about my hours, but he'd probably understand.

"So, now what?" Michael asked.

I looked at him. "Let's get your car out of the ditch and on your way home."

He snorted. "Great."

I understood his sarcasm. From what he had told me, "home" meant couch surfing.

Then I frowned as a new idea stitched itself together. "Michael… I've got an extra room in my apartment. And Bob is always screaming about how we need more drivers. I could put in a good word for you."

He studied my face. "Why would you do that?"

I looked down at the picture of Angie. "Because burdens are always lighter when you have someone there to help you carry them."

I rose and held out my hand to help him up. Then I showed him how to safely hook his car to my truck. A few moments later, the car was up on the road and hitched up for the tow back to town.

But the last thing we did before we left that barren stretch of road was bury my Sig in the ditch. Maybe we could piece together our broken lives, carry the load for one another. But that healing could only happen if I buried that demon where it finally died. And with the sun chasing the last wisps of fog from the air, I drove Mike and his car back to Fremont.

# NOTES ON "BURYING THE DEMON"

DID YOU GET THE idea that this story is about burying a demon?

Round two in 2024, and I'm supposed to write a drama about closure featuring a truck driver. The setting for this one wound up being inspired by a town in southern Minnesota, one where I lived for eight years. It's the sort of place where everyone knows everyone else's business. The plot itself, of a grieving father forgiving his child's killer is one that I've heard many times. Given my former life as a Lutheran pastor, it was a bit too tempting to include a forgiveness arc.

I had a feeling that I leaned into the metaphor of "burying the demon" a bit too much. I really thought this would be it for me. I mean, I had never made it past round two before. So you can imagine my surprise when I learned that I got second place in this heat, meaning I'd go on to the third round!

# Old Orc, New Tricks

THE SPELL DUMPED GORTASH into bright sunshine in a verdant forest. He even spotted two rabbits bounding through the underbrush.

Disgusting.

He adjusted his pack and unclipped the fey cage to check on Pep. The sprite glared at him. He snorted. Like it was his fault transit spells were so rough on fae.

"You got the location?" he prompted.

She pointed. He tried not to brush up against anything as he walked. If he tracked anything pretty into the clan hall after work, he'd catch a tongue-lashing for sure.

Gortash tried to ignore the cheerful birdsong and the sweet scent of flowers, but soon, a headache knotted up behind his sloping brow. If it were up to him, he'd burn it all. Why would anyone in a place this wholesome need his help?

He finally came across a village. A group of sylvan children, green-skinned, mossy-haired, with pointed ears, frolicked in a pasture, but they stopped when they saw him. They fled, screaming the whole way. He ignored them. He wasn't there to fix broken relations between sylvan and orcs.

Pep indicated a small cottage flanked by lush gardens. Gortash tromped over to the front door and banged against the rough wood. No answer.

"Hello?" he bellowed.

Pep made an indignant sound, like breaking glass.

Gortash rolled his eyes, but did what she suggested. He knocked gently. "Dark Wizard Cavalry. How may I assist you today?"

She glared at him. Yeah, he had let some of his annoyance bleed into his tone, but it was a stupid way for an orc to announce himself. He should scream a war cry, weapon in hand, like in the old days.

He caught movement to his right. He whipped around, his hand darting to a sword that hadn't been there for years. Whoever it was ducked behind the bush, then peeked.

"You live here?" Gortash asked.

A kid emerged, and Gortash's eyes narrowed. A human whelp, with dusty blond hair and wide blue eyes. Since when did sylvans let humans live with them?

The boy nodded.

"You know why I was summoned?" Gortash prompted.

Another nod.

"You gonna fill me in, or do I gotta look for your folks?"

The kid's eyes widened even further. He hurried to open the front door. As soon as he did, cold air slithered across Gortash's skin, prickling his arms. Unfocused magik. This was the right place. He squared his shoulders and stepped inside.

Two more kids squatted near a small object in the center of the room. One was a human girl, a little older than the boy. The other was a sylvan boy.

"Kelvin!" the girl snapped at the other human. "What is *he* doing here?"

Kelvin shrugged. "We need help. The thingy's broken."

The girl scowled at him. "But an orc?"

"Makes sense if you think about it," the sylvan boy said. "Orcs have a natural resistance to magik. It stands to reason that—"

"Not now, Daruni." The girl looked at Gortash, hands on her hips. "Well? Can you help us?"

Gortash tamped down the urge to throw her out a window. He kneeled next to the object. A Keldish summoning amulet. He groaned. Someone really needed to recall these. This was the tenth one needing repairs this month.

He looked at the human girl and jerked a thumb at the amulet. "This yours?"

The girl hesitated, uncertainty flickering across her face. Then she stood up straighter. "Yes."

"Uh huh." Gortash leaned in to inspect the problem.

The amulet, a triangular piece of obsidian with silver highlights etched on its surface, vibrated back and forth on the floor. Blue energy crackled along the silver veins. The red gem in the amulet's center flickered. A long crack ran the length of the talisman, snaking around the gem. That had to be the issue. The damage was likely disrupting the flow.

"What were you trying to summon with 'your' amulet? Lich? Archdemon? One of the Nine?" He poked at the amulet, and a spark bit into his finger. He shook his hand, trying to get the feeling back.

The girl stammered. "N-noting in p-particular. W-we weren't all that picky."

He glowered at her. "You activated a summoning amulet without specifying your target? I'm gonna go find your parents and..."

His gaze hitched on something hanging over the fireplace, and his voice trailed off. A massive scimitar, half as long as he was tall, with a jagged blade that seemed to have been forged from darkness. His eyes widened. He knew that weapon.

"Your mother is Helganna?" His voice was little more than a whisper.

The girl turned pale, but she nodded.

"She doesn't want us going through her stuff," the human boy blurted. "But Illie was trying to show off for Daruni and—"

"I wouldn't have if you hadn't dared me to!" Illie shot back.

Gortash held up his hand before the argument spun out of control. He hadn't seen that weapon in years, not since his days in Helganna's brood army. He shuddered, remembering their defeat at the Battle of the Red Tide ten years earlier, shortly before she had disappeared. Who would've thought the Terror of the Sky Realms would settle in a sylvan village and raise a couple of kids?

"Okay, look. I'll fix this, but then you gotta put it back where you found it and never breathe a word about this to anyone. Got it?" He fixed a glare on the sylvan. "You too, pointy."

Daruni opened his mouth to object, but Illie nodded emphatically. Good. He wouldn't have to explain what happened to a retired warlord. Small comfort.

He jerked a thumb toward the door. "Clear out. This'll only take a moment."

Again, Daruni looked ready to object, but Illie snared his hand and dragged both Kelvin and him out the door. Once it was shut, Pep asked a question from her cage, her voice a cascade of skeptical bells.

Gortash snorted. "You're right, I can't fix it. Best I can do is discharge the magik and hope Helganna never notices it's broken."

He unslung his backpack and pulled out his grimoire and the necessary components. Gortash sprinkled some felfiend bile along the crack, dusting it with ground moonadder scales. He slipped on his glasses so he could read the proper incantation, then muttered it.

The amulet stopped shaking, but then a blue light built around it. Gortash bit back a curse. That should've stopped the spell dead, but it looked like the amulet was going to open a portal anyway. Stupid Keldish garbage!

A pillar of smoke erupted from the amulet, swirling through the cabin with the shriek of mountain winds. A figure loomed over Gortash, a creature of abysmal darkness with thick arms, long talons, and prominent horns jutting from his forehead. He flared bat-like wings and roared with a voice that shook the cottage.

"You dare summon me, mortals?" The creature's voice was that of an inferno. "Ask for your boon before I flay the skin from your pitiful bones!"

Gortash rocked back on his heels, gaze still on the amulet. "Hey, Steve."

The demon looked down at him, and his frightening visage melted away. "Oh. Hey, Gortash."

In a flash, the billowing shadows pulled into the demon's body, and he clopped down onto the floor, tucking his leathery wings around him like a cloak. Steve looked down at the amulet and chuckled.

"Another Keldish, huh?" Steve squatted down next to him. "How you been, mate? Work treating you okay?"

Gortash shrugged. "Been better. They gave me a new fae."

"Oh?"

Gortash held up the cage so Steve could peek at Pep. "She's better than the last one."

Pep made what he guessed was an obscene gesture at Steve, who chuckled. The demon looked around the room, and his gaze seemed to linger on the sword.

"Is that what I think it is?"

Gortash nodded.

Steve stood up, smoothing out his shaggy hair and running a hand along both horns. "You seen her yet? Did she mention me?"

"I think she's married."

Steve whirled around, shock radiating across his face. "No!"

"Two kids."

"Ew." Steve straightened up. "Well, if there aren't any mortals who actually need me, I'd better go. Stay safe."

With another blast of smoke, Steve vanished. Gortash glanced at the amulet. It had gone still, although there was a scorch mark surrounding it on the floor. He smirked. Let the kids explain that one. As far as he was concerned, his job was done.

He hefted the cage. "Where to next, Pep?"

Her eyes went vacant for a moment, then she rattled off the next job's details.

Gortash pinched the bridge of his nose. A snapped unicorn bridle? Why did he get all the garbage assignments? He sighed and clipped the cage to his belt and slung his pack over his shoulder. Sure, the world supposedly had become a lot safer, but sometimes he wished he could just smash stuff rather than fix it.

# Notes on "Old Orc, New Tricks"

So, this was my first time in the third round of the NYC Midnight Short Story Challenge. And I was feeling pretty confident going in. My assignment was to write a fantasy story about a dare and a repairman. Fantasy stories are definitely in my wheelhouse.

This time around, I challenged myself by telling a story where many of the details are implied but never really explained fully. I mean, I only had 1,500 words to work with. I thought I did pretty well.

And the twist with Steve! I was chuckling the whole time I wrote that part of the story. Just the silliness of a demon going from "I will kill you and your entire family" to "Want to grab a pint?" was too good to pass up.

The result is my second favorite story in this collection after "Hookah Jones." Unfortunately, as much as I loved this story, it wasn't enough to get me into the final round.

But this story is significant to me in another way. In the fall of 2024, I made a major life change. I became an English teacher. That fall, I reviewed story components with all of my students to make sure that everyone was on the same page. I put together a lecture on plot, characters, point of view, setting, all of it. And then I asked them to read the same short story and dissect it. This is the story I gave them without telling them who the author was.

They all figured it out eventually. But it was a lot of fun to see what my students came up with about theme and all of that.

# THE TRIGGERMAN'S SECRET

LOMBARDO MANOR GLOWERED AT Carlos. He could almost see past the decay to how it might have appeared a hundred years earlier. Bright white walls, soaring pillars, large windows looking out over the expansive grounds. But its heyday had passed. Now the surrounding hills were choked with gnarled trees and waist-high grass. The house wore its age like a giant's skull, the house as dead as the original inhabitant's criminal empire.

"You take me to the nicest places, Professor Valdez."

He twisted to look in the back of the Jeep. Kay Paulson, his research assistant, offered him an impish smile. He fought the urge to wink. Ever since Kay glided into his Roaring '20s course two years ago, they had established a flirtatious, yet chaste, relationship. He could never bring himself to cross that line. He had so little left to lose.

Erik hunched over the wheel, worry etched across his face. "Why do we gotta be here?"

"We need Mr. Lang's permission." Carlos patted Erik on the shoulder. "Let's review: what do we know about Lang?"

"He's rich but weird," Erik murmured.

"Eccentric," Kay corrected.

"Like that Rockefeller guy," Erik said.

Carlos rolled his eyes. "No, like Hearst."

Erik frowned. "What's the difference?"

"Rockefeller gave away his fortune. Hearst kept his urine," Kay said.

Carlos bit back a laugh. "I'm pretty sure Mr. Lang doesn't have a similar collection. Maybe give any drinks he gives us a good sniff. But discreetly. He owns the lake, and we need his permission to go diving."

He and Kay slid out of the Jeep and headed up the steps. Even though the front porch was made of stone, he nearly tripped over the uneven surface. Carlos raised his fist to knock, but before he could, the massive wooden doors opened with a gut-curdling creak. He exchanged a look with Kay, then slipped inside.

The interior of the mansion looked little better than the exterior. Everything was coated with a thick layer of dust and cobwebs, except for a path scuffed clean down the middle of the hall. Light flickered through an open doorway.

"Hello? Mr. Lang? You here?" he called.

He rounded the corner and stepped into an enormous library. Hundreds of books lined the walls, and most of the furniture was covered with tarps. But a solitary figure sat in a plush chair near a guttering fire. The man appeared as ancient as the house itself, little more than skin and bones with wispy white hair. The old man looked up at him with rheumy eyes.

"Professor Valdez. So good of you to come."

"Good of you to meet with us." He turned and motioned for Kay and Erik to join him.

Lang rocked in his chair, as if getting ready to stand, but couldn't quite make it. Kay rushed forward and shook his hand, introducing herself and Erik. The old man settled back in his chair.

"I must say, I'm a bit confused why you're so eager to go diving in my lake, Professor," Lang said. "I hope you don't mind explaining it to me again."

Carlos ground his teeth. He had already explained this, both over the phone and in writing. But clearly Lang was a little senile.

"I'm sure you're aware of who built this house, Mr. Lang," Carlos said.

Lang nodded. "Ezekiel Lombardo. I believe they called him 'The Trigger-man,' yes? Fairly powerful, if I recall correctly."

That was one way of putting it. Lombardo had been one of the most powerful mob bosses in Kansas City during Prohibition. According to Carlos's research, Lombardo had controlled just about everything, from rum-running to prostitution and everything in between.

Carlos held out a hand to Kay, who handed him a black-and-white photo, one of the only known photos of Lombardo. He was broad in the shoulders, wearing a pinstriped suit and a fedora. Lombardo clutched a walking stick in one hand, with a large skull for a handle. Carlos showed it to Lang, who reached for it with trembling hands.

"Lombardo came to Kansas City in December 1919, and within a month, he controlled every criminal organization. Nobody knows how he did it," Carlos said.

"And you have a theory how?" Lang asked.

Carlos gritted his teeth. He glanced at Kay, who nodded, her eyes bright and encouraging.

"I do. I think he used magick."

Lang looked up at him, his face pinching into a frown. Carlos held his breath. He hadn't mentioned this to the old man yet. Usually, this prompted laughter, not support.

"Go on."

Breathing a quick sigh of relief, Carlos tapped the picture. "I believe Lombardo's cane is an artifact known as the *Umbri dâ Morti*, something created by Pope John XII in the tenth century CE. It shows up in Sicilian folklore now and then, but the last explicit reference to it says Arnestu Lombardo used it in the seventeenth century to destroy his rivals. According to my research, Ezekiel was a direct descendant of Arnestu."

Lang's face pinched into a frown. "And you think this—"

"*Umbri dâ Morti*," Kay supplied helpfully.

"—is in my lake?"

Carlos held out a hand, and Kay handed him the journal. "I do. I acquired this journal, which was kept by Bernie Gatson, one of Lombardo's bodyguards. Apparently Lombardo was having an affair with Abigail, Bernie's sister, who worked here as a maid. She wanted to escape Lombardo, but felt she couldn't unless they got rid of his cane. According to the last entry, Bernie wrote he was going to toss it in the lake behind Lombardo's mansion."

Lang's gaze sharpened. "So what happened to Bernie?"

"No one really knows." He reached for Kay again, who handed him a letter preserved in a plastic sleeve. "But last year, I found this letter, written by Bernie's wife to her cousin a few years later, saying how Abigail showed up the night Bernie disappeared, hysterical and sobbing, saying that her brother had 'done it' but that he had died in the process."

With the same trembling hand, Lang took the letter and looked it over. Carlos held his breath. There was so much more he could have said. How Sicilian folklore said that only water could dampen the *Umbri dâ Morti's* power. How Lombardo, who had been all but untouchable for years, was killed by one of Tom Pendergast's cronies within days of Bernie's disappearance. It all added up, at least to Carlos. But would Lang buy any of it?

Lang looked over the letter and the journal. He coughed several times, a deep rattle, before handing them back.

"Professor Valdez, you have my permission to search the lake."

Carlos wanted to whoop. He turned to Kay, who beamed at him. Finally! He was finally going to prove his theory. He would finally prove to the world that he wasn't crazy.

"How much longer is this gonna take?" Erik asked.

Carlos gritted his teeth. "No idea."

He hunched over the screen of the metal detector, willing it to find the cane. They had been searching the lake for most of the day, slowing dragging a probe through the water. He hadn't realized how large the lake truly was, at least half a mile long and a quarter mile wide. If they didn't find something soon, they'd have to come back the next day. He would, but—

There! A solitary blip on the screen. He turned to the others and gave a thumbs-up. Kay cut the trawling motor and quickly dropped anchor. Erik fiddled with the SCUBA tank at his feet.

"You sure we won't see anything down there?" he asked. "What if Lombardo dumped bodies in here? You know, with cement shoes?"

Carlos chuckled. "He wouldn't do that in his own backyard. Now c'mon, let's get going. We don't have much light left."

The three of them quickly put on their gear. Carlos was the first into the lake, surprised at how cold the water was as it swallowed him. Within a minute, both Erik and Kay had followed him in. He signaled for them to head down.

By the time they reached the bottom, darkness had consumed them. A shiver wormed through Carlos. By his calculations, the lake was sixty feet deep, which meant there wouldn't be much natural light. But this felt darker and far colder than it should have been. He quickly pulled a light from his belt and switched it on.

A gaunt face, its mouth open in a scream, flashed in front of him.

He choked on his air, then fumbled with the light before bringing it up. Nothing but weeds swaying in the wake of his frantic motions. An entire underwater forest, by the looks of it. He had never seen such thick growth at the bottom of a lake before. Carlos took a few deeper breaths to calm his heart, then handed the light to Kay before pulling out an underwater metal detector. He switched it on and heard a faint ping as it picked up what was hopefully the *Umbri dâ Morti*.

Navigating the tangle of weeds proved difficult. It felt like hands clawing at him as he searched through the murky darkness. But then he spotted a glinting reflection of Kay's light just in front of him. He darted forward, pushing aside the tangled weeds and...

There it was, stuck in the lake's silt, two feet of wood with an ornate bronze top in the shape of a skull, its mouth open in a smiling rictus. The wood appeared completely intact, which surprised him. He would have thought it would have rotted by now. More evidence it was a magickal artifact! Carlos fought to keep from laughing in triumph.

Carlos passed the metal detector to Erik and planted his feet on the sandy bottom. He tugged at the cane, but it was stuck. He grunted and strained, but it wouldn't budge. Finally, though, with some twisting and wiggling, he pulled the cane free. He turned, holding it up in triumph for the others to see. Kay's eyes beamed at him, and she gave him a thumbs up. Erik, though, shied away, almost drifting into the swaying weeds...

Spectral hands burst from the weeds, grabbing at his arms and legs.

Carlos's eyes went wide as shadowy hands tore at Erik, slicing through his skin. Erik thrashed, trying to get free, but one clawed hand cut his air tube. Bubbles burst for the surface and Erik tried to free himself, but the hands pulled him back into the weeds. He screamed, the sound muffled by the water. But then his voice cut off.

More spectral forms emerged from the surrounding weeds. Carlos kicked forward, snaring Kay by the hand. He dragged her up and away. They broke the surface thirty feet from the boat. Carlos frowned. Why was it so dark? Had the sun already set? That didn't make sense. They hadn't been down there that long...

No, focus! He could somehow feel movement beneath him in the lake. Those things were coming for them. He swam frantically for the boat, but he couldn't move as quickly as Kay since he was carrying the cane. He wasn't about to let that go, not now that he had found it! She clambered over the side a moment before he did.

"What happened to Erik?" Kay shrieked. "What were those things?"

"I don't know." Carlos's voice was a gasp. "I don't know! Start the motor!"

Kay turned to the big outboard motor. The water around the boat frothed as shadowy creatures burst from the lake. They almost looked human, their faces like desiccated corpses. He thought one might be wearing the tattered remnants of a zoot suit, but he didn't want to look too closely. The creatures rocked the boat as they pulled themselves over the edge. Carlos shouted and swung the cane, trying to drive them off, but it passed through them harmlessly.

Kay screamed. Carlos whirled just in time to see three of the monstrosities latch onto her arms and shoulder, dragging her out of the boat and into the water. Her voice fell silent.

Carlos turned in a frantic circle, waiting for the monsters to attack him. But they didn't. They hovered above the water, circling the boat, snarling at him. They were vaguely human-shaped, although their bodies tapered off into insubstantial wisps. Their eyes glowed with a burning menace he could feel.

He glanced at the cane. Was that why they didn't attack? Maybe. Best not wait around to find out. He fired up the motor and sped back to the landing. The boat bounced as it slammed through the rough water. Carlos risked a glance over his shoulder. The specters followed him, stretching their spindly fingers after him.

As he approached the shore, he saw a figure standing near the Jeep. It looked like...Mr. Lang? He shouted a warning, but the elderly man didn't seem to hear him. Then the boat slid up onto the shore. Carlos vaulted out of the boat.

"Mr. Lang! We have to get out of here. There are...there are *things* in the water!"

The old man still didn't seem to hear him. He toddled forward, his eyes on the cane.

"So you found it, did you?" Lang asked.

Lang reached out with a trembling hand and plucked the cane from Carlos's numb fingers. He looked up and down its length, a wide smile splitting his face.

"I must commend you, Professor. I've been searching for this for years and never thought it would be so close."

Carlos stumbled back a step, but then he heard the splashing behind him and froze.

"In all your research, you missed some vital details. How Abigail Gatson was pregnant with Ezekiel's child when she fled the mansion. Or that a person with Lombardo blood can only truly wield the Umbri dâ Morti." Lang's face lit up with malicious glee. "Someone like Abigail's son. Someone like me."

Carlos started to say something, but then powerful hands latched onto his arms and legs. He thrashed, trying to free himself, but there were too many of them and they were too strong. Pain burned through his arms and legs, multiple stabs and slices deep in his flesh. Carlos tried to cry out, but the darkness flooded his lungs, and all he could do was whimper.

As the specters dragged him back into the lake, one final thought pierced through the agony. He had been right. He had been right all along. But unfortunately, he would take that to a watery grave.

# Notes on "The Triggerman's Secret"

On to the 2025 short story challenge, and the first round assignment tied me up in creative knots. I had to write a horror story about a hypothesis and a SCUBA diver. I remember reading those prompts and my mind going completely blank.

I went through a few different ideas on how to bring it all together. One idea was about a group of researchers doing an experiment on an alien artifact that had to be submerged in water for their own safety, and how they would have to dive to the object to study it. I actually started writing that version of the story, only to realize I had no idea where it was going and I was wasting precious time spinning my wheels. I scrapped it and went back to the drawing board.

This story came together in something of a panic. I knew I had to do something scary. I knew there had to be a SCUBA diver. I knew there had to be a hypothesis. In a fit of frantic inspiration, I slammed this one together and sent it off. Much to my surprise, I made it to the next round.

# BLIND SPOT

Mr. Erickson glares as I slide behind the driver's seat. "Jessica. You're late."

I grimace. "I know, but it wasn't my fault! Laney Price was showing me this new skirt she found at a garage sale last week, and—"

He clicks his pen and jots down a note on his clipboard.

Never mind then. I put on my seatbelt, then make sure Mr. Erickson is buckled in too. He isn't, but when he sees me check, he nods and does so. I then move the seat up—someone really tall had driven the driver's ed car before me—adjust the mirrors, start the engine, and check the dashboard for any indicator lights. With each step, Mr. Erickson makes a large check on the form. I hazard a bare grin. So far, so good.

My phone buzzes in my purse. I freeze, shooting a glance at Mr. Erickson. His pen hovers over the clipboard, his gaze sharpening.

"May I?" I ask. "I'm not actually driving."

He sighs, but waves for me to go ahead.



I wince. I had made plans with Naomi, my best friend, to go thrifting at Rags Recycled, our favorite clothing boutique, but I had forgotten about this lesson. With my test just two weeks away, I need the practice.

Three dots cycle, then disappear, then cycle again. I frown. What's taking so long for her to reply?

> kk miss u

My frown deepens. What does that mean? We just saw each other in AP Bio only an hour ago.

My phone buzzes as another text comes in, this one from my other best friend, Kevin.

> Planning on going to RR today?

Why would he ask that? He hates shopping, especially for clothes.

Mr. Erickson clears his throat. I hand him my phone and he drops it in the glove compartment. "Drive us over to the lot so we can practice parallel parking."

I nod. Maybe this isn't as fun as finding the perfect vintage outfit, but once I have my license, Naomi and I can go shopping whenever we want. Not a bad deal, even if it means spending time with Mr. Erickson.

The car shudders as Mr. Erickson rummages in the trunk. I lean on the steering wheel, waiting for him to set up the cones. My gaze skitters across the empty lot. I feel insulted that we're practicing here. I've driven on the streets plenty of times. I mean, sure, I did almost rear end that old lady last time. And I missed our exit on the freeway the time before that. But to use cones in a parking lot? Please.

My gaze lands on the glove compartment. I could see if I have any new messages. Why was everyone asking about RR?

I mean, I get it. I love RR. They have the best stuff. One time, I found a complete stewardess uniform from the '60s in near-perfect condition. Great little skirt, perfect blazer, a paisley cravat that just brought it all together, and the whole thing only cost thirty bucks! When I wore it to school, Drake noticed me right away. That's why I wanted to go to RR with Naomi today. With prom coming up, I'm sure Drake's going to ask me to go. Rumor has it he's brewing up the perfect promposal, and I just know we could find the perfect outfit for when he asks.

A knock on the window. I whip around. Mr. Erickson motions for me to roll down the window.

"The cones aren't in there," he says. "We're going to have to find somewhere else to practice."

My mind zings as the obvious answer occurs to me. How about we get a two-for-one? "I know just the place."

The drive's tense. Every few minutes, Mr. Erickson scribbles something on his clipboard. But within ten minutes, I turn the corner and there it is: Rags Recycled. My oasis, my Mecca, my own secret garden. The building itself isn't much to look at. I think it was an old train station at one point, painted white, although the color has faded and most of it is falling off. It's just dingy enough to scare away people from the bargains within. And just as I expected, there's a gap between two of the parked cars just big enough for the driver's ed car.

Mr. Erickson spots it too. "Pull in there."

I nod and creep down the road, my mind frantic. I know the real reason he wanted to practice in the lot. Every time I've tried to parallel park, I wind up hitting a cone. He probably thinks I'm not ready to do this in the "real world" yet. But I have to, right?

I pull forward, stopping when my passenger-side mirror lines up with the other car. I crank the wheel to the right and put the car in reverse, slowly inching into the spot. Mr. Erickson cranes around in his seat to watch my progress. He grunts, but it's an approving sound. I grip the steering wheel a little tighter and straighten out, tapping the brake with enough room between me and the car behind us to spare. I did it!

Mr. Erickson turns to me, the barest smile on his face. "Good job."

I look past him at RR. First chance I get, I'm going to find that perfect outfit for Drake's promposal and—

The door to RR swings open and Naomi sashays out. Her face is bright, and I recognize her expression. She found something good in there. But she's not carrying anything. Where are her purchases?

Then Drake exits, carrying two large paper bags. He smiles at Naomi, who beams up at him. Then she pops up on her tiptoes and he leans down and—

And he kisses her.

My stomach twists, and my clammy hands tighten on the steering wheel. Is *this* why she texted, to make sure I wouldn't be here? She knows how much I like Drake!

Mr. Erickson, oblivious to the storm raging inside me, scratches down a few more notes. "All right, Jessica, why don't you pull out now?"

Gladly. I don't want to be here. With no hesitation, I yank on the wheel and hit the gas.

"Did you check your blind spots before you—" Mr. Erickson's voice pitches up as the car lurches into the lane.

Something thumps into the car right next to me. I scream and slam on the brakes, the car jutting into the road. Mr. Erickson tears open the door and rushes around the car. I sit frozen in my seat, trying to control my breathing, feeling the sweat pour down my back. I hit something!

I force myself to look. A bicycle lies in the road, someone sprawled out next to it. He rolls over as Mr. Erickson approaches, and my eyes widen. It's Kevin! Did I actually hit him with my car? He looks up at me, and I freeze. There's a large gash along his forehead, probably from where his head hit the pavement. Similar scrapes dot his elbows and his jeans have torn open as well. Mr. Erickson helps him to his feet, and he wobbles, but then steadies himself.

People gather around the car, and I spot Naomi and Drake standing at the front of the crowd. Drake is so focused on Kevin that he doesn't notice me.

But Naomi does. Her face goes pale, but when Drake motions for her to leave, Naomi offers me a shrug and follows.

I groan. Could this day possibly get any worse?

Turns out, it could.

Mr. Erickson was not happy. When my parents came to get me, he berated them and me about my lack of focus, saying I wasn't ready for my test and we'd need to pay for the damages.

Thankfully, my parents didn't go completely ballistic. They listened to my side of the story, and Mom at least seemed sympathetic about what happened with Naomi and Drake. Dad wasn't. He lectured me on priorities and safety, saying I'll have to reimburse them for the damage. About the only good thing was that they didn't ground me. They didn't have to. When we got home, I just went up to my room.

After doomscrolling for three hours, I groan and let the phone drop to the floor. How could things have gone so badly so quickly? How could I go to school tomorrow?

A gentle knock at the door. I look up, expecting Mom. Instead, Kevin pokes his head in.

"You okay?" he asks.

Tears sting my eyes. "What about you?"

He steps into the room, and my gaze locks on the bandages taped to his forehead and wrapped around his elbows.

"I've been better."

I groan and flop onto the bed. He steps over and sits on the edge, then places something next to me. It's a cup of frozen yogurt from the shop next to RR. My favorite.

"Thought you could use a treat," he said.

I really don't, but it looks so good I can't help myself. Kevin offers a spoon, and I take it, savoring the cool strawberry taste as it dances across my tongue.

"So, Naomi and Drake," Kevin says.

I wince. "Yeah."

"Did you know?"

I shake my head. "Did you?"

He nods sheepishly. "I overheard him talking in English. Said he was taking Naomi shopping, and he was going to ask her to prom while they were at RR. That's why I texted you. I wanted to warn you."

I swallow a groan. That was our spot, Naomi's and mine. And now, anytime I went there, I'd only remember what she did. What they both did.

But a question prickles my mind. "Then why were you there?"

"Because...because, well, I wanted to get you something."

He produces a small bag and pulls out a diaphanous scarf, pastel and exquisite. I gasp as the fabric slides between my fingers, which snag on the price tag, and I check it.

"You paid twenty for this?"

He smiles, a twinkle in his eye. "No, five. They gave me a discount because... well..."

My cheeks heat. "Why would you get me this?"

He rubs a hand on the back of his neck, grimacing. I frown. I've never seen him at a loss for words before.

"Because I know you'd look good wearing it. Especially if you wore it to prom." He meets my gaze. "With me."

I freeze, suddenly as cold as the frozen yogurt. Go to prom...with Kevin? I mean, I had never thought about that.

He stammers, and words start pouring out of him. "I mean, I know this is out of nowhere, and I also know you were hoping for a big, TikTok-worthy promposal. But I've been giving this a lot of thought and I...really want to go to prom. With you, I mean. And maybe see what happens? Unless you're worried about our friendship, but I think we could have something good here."

Did I see him that way? I never had before, but as I thought about it, I realized maybe he had always been in my blind spot. And maybe it was time for me to really see him.

A smile tickles my lips. I drop the scarf and the spoon and snare his hands. He stops and looks up at me.

"I'd love to," I whisper.

He smiles, his expression shaky, but then an impish light glimmers in his eyes. "Well, good. I mean, you kind of owe me after hitting me with a car."

I swat his arm. Maybe this wasn't the way I expected things to go, but hey, going to prom with my best friend, who might be more? Talk about a great bargain.

# NOTES ON "BLIND SPOT"

This one has a special place in my heart for a very weird reason.

The second round of 2025 gave me the prompts of a romance about a blind spot and a bargain hunter. So I made a teenage romance about a bargain-hunting girl who struggles with a literal and metaphorical blind spot.

Rags Recycled and Jessica's love for off-beat vintage clothing was inspired by a childhood friend of mine. In high school, my friend Beth would go to a store in Minneapolis called Ragstock where she found all sorts of unique clothing items. She once came to school in a vintage Air Force dress uniform. It worked for her in a way I doubt it could have worked for anyone else.

Once I was done with the story, I thought it was pretty good. The judges disagreed, and that was that for 2025.

So why do I love this story so much? Because of what I named the characters. But to explain that, I need to rewind the clock to 2016.

Back in 2016, my family moved to the Kansas City area from Minnesota for my job. A tiny factor in that move was the possibility that I might take part in a homeschool writing workshop for high schoolers called One Year Adventure Novel. A bunch of my friends taught there every summer, and it always looked like fun. After my family moved, one of them got me in contact with the organizer, a man named Dan Schwabauer. He graciously invited me to teach.

So in the summer of 2016, I went to my first OYAN summer workshop. In my first teaching session, I told the students a story about how a friend of mine once asked me to read the manuscript for a romance novel that she had written. I threw in an offhand joke about how that figured since "when you think romance, you think John Otte."

This is where I learned something about OYAN Summer Workshop participants: give them a joke, and they will run with it. This became a meme. It's been ten years since that class, and that phrase persists.

But there's more to it than that. In that original lecture, I was discussing conflict in story, and I showed two techniques to ramp up conflict in fiction. To do so, I came up with a lame romantic story about two young people, best friends, but one of them wants to escape the friend zone. I told three different versions of their story in the lecture. The names of these characters? Jessica and Kevin.

Dear reader, these two have become part of the meme. The students have encouraged me to write a love story for Jessica and Kevin almost every year.

So you can imagine their shock and delight when, at the 2025 OYAN Summer Workshop, I shared some of the feedback I got from the judges on this story in which they complimented my ability to write romantic stories and the students noticed what the name of the young lovers in "Blind Spot" were.

Pure pandemonium.

That's part of the reason this story is included in this book. I promised them that someday they'd be able to read it for themselves. That day has come.

# THE BUTCHER OF MLADICE

ROMAN'S MAMKA ALWAYS SAID if he was ever in trouble, he should find her. His tati told him a real man fights when he has no choice. But standing in the railway station, with soldiers approaching him, he knew he couldn't do either. Mamka had died when he was a baby. And Tati, he had disappeared the night the bad men came to Mladice, the night Tati had pushed him under the bed and told him to stay there, no matter what he heard. Without his parents to help or fight for him, what was left for Roman to do but run?

So he did, darting down onto the tracks. The men shouted, but Roman ignored them. He dove underneath a car, dragging himself across the rough gravel. Sharp pain lanced through his knees, enough that tears formed in his eyes. But he bit his lip to keep from crying. Couldn't let them hear him!

What could he do now? Coming here had seemed like such a good idea. Tati always told him how the trains crisscrossed the land, taking people anywhere they wanted to go. So when Roman realized his home was empty, he had gone to Breznice to find the train that would take him somewhere safe. What he found instead were grownups milling about, all as scared as Roman. And soldiers everywhere, wearing their green clothes, pushing and yelling and cursing.

A hand grasped at his foot. Roman's gaze met the scowl of a soldier who groped for Roman's leg. He kicked at him, then scrambled away. Trains loomed over him. Cargo, passenger, tanker, so many cars, so many places he could hide. But where could he go where the soldiers wouldn't find him?

There! A passenger train's metal wheels groaned against the tracks. One door hadn't been closed all the way. Roman clambered up onto the steps and shoved it open, slipping inside and pulling the door behind him. He crawled up the stairs and peeked down the long hallway. A man in a black uniform stood at the opposite end of the car, speaking to someone in the room.

Roman bit his lower lip, frowning as he thought. Maybe he could find a place to hide in a room like that? Maybe. He was small. All the kids in Mladice had called him "runt." Tati had said he'd eventually grow, but now? Maybe being small would help.

While the man in the uniform was distracted, Roman crept down the hall. But he didn't make it far. The man turned in his direction, so Roman slipped into the nearest room. He watched the door, holding his breath, hoping that the man wouldn't look in here.

"Hello? Who are you?"

Roman froze, then turned around. An old man sat on a bench, staring at him with wide brown eyes. He wore a rumpled brown coat. With his neatly trimmed white beard, Roman might have mistaken him for someone's kindly grandfather, but his gaze stopped at the scar that slithered from the man's beard and past his left eye. Roman's breath turned ragged as he stared.

"Do you have a name, boy?" The man's gravelly voice sent a shiver down Roman's spine, but then he leaned forward and held out a hand to him. "Don't worry. I'm a friend."

Roman's feet felt like they had been glued to the floor. He wanted to do what the man said. Tati had always told him to do what his elders said, that it was important he be a good boy and obedient. But staring at the man with the scar, he could barely breathe.

Then the door behind him rattled open. "What is going on in here?"

The man in the uniform glared down at Roman. He looked like one of the avenging angels Tati used to speak of in hushed tones when he showed him pictures in that book he kept hidden under his mattress.

But then the man with the scar spoke up. "This is my nephew. I told you I was traveling with him, yes?"

The man in uniform looked angry, but then the scarred man rose and stepped around Roman, blocking him from the man's view. "Our arrangement is so inflexible, is it, that it may not admit one more?"

After a bit of grumbling, the man in uniform shut the door. The scarred man turned to Roman and smiled. With the scar, his expression looked more like pain than friendliness.

"Small men like to cling to whatever power they have, even as the world crumbles around them."

Roman swallowed and nodded. What else could he do?

The man sat down and motioned for Roman to come near. "But if you are going to be my nephew, I should know your name."

He hesitated. Tati always said strangers couldn't be trusted. But what choice did he really have? "Roman."

"Ah, a powerful name. Rich. Ironic. You know the history of our proud Soravia, yes? We started as an outpost for the Roman Empire, founded by Marcus Aurelius himself. As empires rose and fell, Soravia stood proud." He slumped onto the bench, looking suddenly tired. "Too proud for our own good, it turns out."

What could Roman say to that? He stepped closer. "What is your name?"

The man considered him. "You may call me Uncle Jakub. We will travel together, yes?" He rummaged in his pocket and pulled out a candy wrapped in wax paper. He held it out, a scant grin on his face.

Roman stared at the treat, and his stomach lurched. He suddenly remembered he hadn't eaten anything since the night Tati hid him under the bed. His hesitation was short-lived. He snatched the candy and unwrapped it, revealing a dull green taffy. Roman stuffed it into his mouth, gobbling it in two bites. After swallowing the last bit, he looked at Jakub, his eyes wide. He wanted more, but it didn't seem polite to ask.

Jakub chuckled, fishing another sweet out of his pocket and handing it over. Then he slowly kneeled down, nodding toward Roman's knee. "Let's get that cleaned up, shall we?"

Roman looked down and realized that blood seeped through his pant leg. Jakub gently rolled up his pant leg, making a soft clucking sound as he did. Then the old man pulled out a handkerchief and carefully tied the white material around Roman's knee.

The old man nodded. "There we go. Not too bad. Should heal quickly enough."

As Roman unwrapped the next taffy, his gaze traced Jakub's scar. "How did that happen?"

The old man's smile faltered. "Grenade. The Nazis nearly took my eye in '39. Because I lived, they gave me this." He pulled something out of his other pocket, looking down at it as he turned it over and over in his hand. Then he held it out to Roman.

It was a medal, a sword surrounded by a wreath, both cast in bronze. The attached fabric, a white stripe bordered by red, was tattered and faded.

Jakub jerked his chin at it. "With gratitude for serving our nation." His voice turned wistful. "Service that maybe should have ended then, perhaps."

"So you're a hero," Roman whispered, handing the medal back to Jakub.

The old man started to say something, but then clamped his mouth shut. Instead, he retrieved the medal and tucked it away, then sat down and patted the seat next to him.

Roman clambered onto the bench, settling in next to Jakub. The clacking rhythm of the train gently rocked him, and before long, he drifted off to sleep.

A loud screech jerked Roman out of his nap. He thrashed for a moment. Where was he? Where was Tati? Then it came back to him: the train yard, the soldiers, meeting Jakub. He looked up at his new uncle. He expected to see the older man smiling down at him, maybe offering him another taffy.

Instead, Jakub stared out the window. His forehead glistened with sweat; his hands clenched in his lap.

"What is it?" Roman murmured.

At first, Jakub didn't seem to hear him. His lips moved, but no sound came out. Then he whirled on Roman, his eyes wide. Roman flinched away, suddenly scared.

"Remember what we told the conductor?" he whispered. "You are my nephew. I am your dear Uncle Jakub, yes?"

Roman nodded, transfixed by the strange light in Jakub's eyes.

"Good boy! And we are traveling together, yes? Heading to East Berlin to visit your mother."

"But Mamka died." What was the word Tati had used? "She starved right after I was born."

Jakub stared at him, his face twisting into a strange expression. Like he was mad and sad at the same time. Roman didn't like it. He shied away.

"Fine. We're visiting...my sister. Your dear Auntie Anja, understand?"

Roman shook his head. He didn't have an Auntie Anja. Tati had said that his only uncle had moved to Breznice because he had to work in the mines.

Then Jakub grabbed Roman by the arms, squeezing tightly. "I need you to do this for me, Roman. I lied for you, yes? When the conductor came? I was your hero then, yes?"

He pulled out the medal and pressed it into Roman's hand. The sword's tip bit into Roman's skin.

"I need you to be my hero now, understand?"

He didn't, but he nodded anyway. Jakub blew out a sharp breath and released him, quickly smoothing out his coat. He offered Roman a wink and leaned back on the bench.

They sat there in tense silence. Then the door slid open, revealing three men in the green soldier clothes. Two had rifles in their hands. The third, shorter than the others, still seemed to loom over them. The short one stepped into the room, then pulled a photograph from his breast pocket. He held it up, looked between it and Jakub, and smiled. It wasn't pleasant. Roman found it hard to breathe. The room felt much too small for three people staring at each other.

"So we've found you," he said, his voice high and reedy. "Trying to slink off, *tovarisch*? What would your people think, their leader trying to flee to Germany while Soravia burns?"

Jakub shook his head, but then slowly reached into his coat, pulling out a wad of papers. His hand trembling as he did. "I-I do not know what you mean. My name is Jakub Marousek. I am traveling to East Berlin with my nephew to visit my sister."

The soldier didn't take them. "Oh, come now. Do you think such forgeries'd fool us? We know who you are, Eduard Zdenek. Hero of Soravia. Leader of the People." The soldier's smile sharpened. "The Butcher of Mladice. Did you think you could escape after killing all those people?"

After he what? Roman looked up at Jakub, his eyes wide. Sweat dripped down the old man's brow. He glanced at Roman, fear burning in his eyes.

"I heard of that, yes." Jakub's voice quavered as he spoke. "Nasty business. You think—"

*Crack!* The soldier slapped Jakub across the cheek. Roman squeaked, flinching.

"Nikita Sergeyevich trusted you to keep the Soravians in line, and you failed. You will come with us to Moscow to answer to him."

The old man turned to Roman, his eyes pleading. "Tell them, Roman. Tell them who I am. I am your Uncle Jakub, yes?"

Roman looked from him to the soldier, who stared at him expectantly. He squeezed his fists tight, feeling the tip of the sword cut into his palm, and he remembered the taste of the taffy.

He sat up straight, feeling the weight of the medal in his hand. Mamka had told him to find her when he was in trouble. Tati had told him to fight when he had no choice.

Roman's fingers slowly unclenched, and he opened his mouth.

# Notes on "The Butcher of Mladice"

A NEW YEAR, A new puzzle to figure out. The first round of 2026 was a thriller about a stowaway and a status symbol.

I had an initial idea that I really liked: I wanted to tell the story of a servant girl in a palace. She's an outcast because either she was a thief or her parents were (I hadn't quite nailed that down). She had a crush on the son of the local wine merchant, but she'd never be able to act on her feelings because of her past. One day, the aforementioned son delivers a bunch of wine to the palace. Why? Because the king was entertaining a powerful archmage, an aloof and cruel man. As the girl brings in the casks, she discovers a stowaway in one. It's a young boy, one who claims that the archmage is a fraud. He says he wants the servant girl to prove it by breaking into the archmage's quarters, promising that if she does this, he'll pay her back by removing a brand on her cheek that marks her as a thief or the daughter of thieves.

The girl goes ahead, and breaks in, only to be caught. She's brought before the king, who condemns her to death for her crimes. Before she can be executed, people in the court object, saying that the archmage should carry out the execution using the powers granted to him by the amulet he wears, the one that marks him as the archmage. The archmage demurs, saying he won't stoop so low, but when the crowd insists, he tries...only nothing happens. The amulet does nothing.

The young boy emerges from the crowd and reveals that he is the actual archmage and that the man with the amulet is an impostor who stole the amulet. The king orders the impostor executed; the true archmage uses his powers to remove the girl's brand, and she goes off to find the wine merchant's son.

I really liked this story. Only there was a slight problem: how would I fit all of this into 2,000 words?

I had started writing this fantasy thriller, only to realize I would run out of words much too quickly. So I tried cutting the wine merchant's son. I realized that wouldn't be enough. So reluctantly, I went back to the drawing board.

My next idea was similar, with a princess discovering a stowaway on a sailing vessel who encouraged her to... And I quickly realized that that idea would be just as long and complicated and wouldn't work either.

So what to do? Well, what about a stowaway on a train? I had just listened to a podcast about Miloš Jakeš and the Prague Spring of 1968. Suddenly I had the idea of a little boy fleeing his home in a fictional Eastern European country and winding up in the same train car with an old man who is also trying to flee.

The challenge of this story was Roman's point of view. I know what happened to Roman's parents and why, but I quickly realized that Roman wouldn't understand anything about geopolitics or the atrocities that consumed his family. I would have to drop hints about it and hope for the best.

As for the ending, I borrowed a page from Frank Stockton's "The Lady, or the Tiger?" What did Roman do? I really don't know. What do you think?

I don't know if I made it to the next round of the 2026 Short Story Challenge. As I'm writing this, I have several weeks of waiting before I'll find out. Fingers crossed.

# Project PanOptic

Aegis hated places like this.

The bar was in an apartment building's basement, half a level below the street. The whole thing was wedged between a shuttered laundromat and a payday loan office that still had a flickering neon sign, guttering like a dying pulse. The windows were narrow and grimy; the glass tinted so dark it barely mattered that it was still technically daytime. Inside, the air smelled like stale beer, ozone from cheap electronics, and desperation that had soaked into the walls over decades.

She kept her powers suppressed as she moved, letting herself look smaller than she really was. She wore a hooded jacket two sizes too big over her uniform. The patrons' eyes slid off her as she crossed the room. Good.

*The best trick is to hide in plain sight,* mija. *You can strike harder and faster that way.*

A shiver wormed down her spine at his voice. Would she ever be free of those echoes?

Her contact sat in a corner booth beneath a busted light fixture, hunched over a glass of some amber liquid. He was older than she'd expected, but worn down in a way that came from knowing too much and being paid too little to forget it. His left hand twitched every few seconds, fingers tapping an anxious rhythm against the tabletop.

She slid into the booth across from him.

"You're late," he muttered without looking up.

Aegis grunted in what she hoped sounded gruff and menacing. "I'm careful."

That got his attention. He looked up, eyes sharp despite the drink. She held his gaze, hoping that he wouldn't figure out the real reason she was late. Her high school had only just let out half an hour ago. And she had to take the time to change. Bad enough she had to come here, but if she had shown up as Marisol Reyes instead of Aegis, she would have been laughed out the door.

"You alone?" he prompted.

"Yes."

A pause. A breath. "Good."

When the waiter came over, she didn't bother ordering anything. Not just because she was underage. She didn't trust any of the glasses to be all that clean.

The informant leaned back, studying her like he was trying to decide whether she was worth the trouble. "You didn't tell me what this was about when you reached out."

"You told me not to," she said. "Don't trust phones or texting or email. Only speak face to face, remember?"

His lips twitched. "Yeah, I guess so. That's good advice, especially what I've learned."

Silence stretched between them. Somewhere behind the bar, glasses clinked. A sports game murmured on a TV no one was watching.

Finally, he sighed. "You asked about Nexora."

She said nothing, just gave a curt nod.

"And Project PanOptic."

Again, she let her silence speak for her. *The big dog doesn't have to bark,* mija. *Everyone knows to fear its bite.* Her lip twitched at the unneeded memory.

His fingers stopped tapping. He took a slow drink, then set the glass down with deliberate care.

"Who sent you?" he asked.

"No one."

"That's almost never true."

No need to respond to that. He was fishing, and they both knew it.

The informant exhaled. "PanOptic isn't what they're telling the press."

Aegis snorted. "I already knew that."

He quirked a brow at her.

"It's more than just software," Aegis went on.

That made him flinch. He glanced toward the bar, then leaned forward, lowering his voice. "You didn't hear that from me."

"I haven't heard anything yet."

He reached into his jacket and slid something across the table. A flash drive. "That has schematics, internal memos, and security routing for Nexora's main campus. Not the stuff they show investors. The stuff they bury."

Aegis was tempted to palm the drive right then and there, but she held back. The moment she accepted that drive, the meeting would end. "So what is PanOptic?"

He hesitated. "It's...a convergence point. Data from everywhere—cameras, satellites, biometric feeds, social media, traffic systems. All of it flows into one place."

"And then?"

"And then it sees," he said quietly.

A chill crawled up her spine.

"You said it's not just software," she prompted.

"There's a core component. Proprietary. One of a kind."

"Hardware?"

"Yes," he said, then corrected himself. "Sort of."

"Can it be replaced?"

He shook his head. "Not easily. Not quickly. If it's destroyed, PanOptic goes dark. For years. Maybe forever."

"This core component. Where is it?"

"Second floor. Main R&D lab. Locked behind more security than the rest of the building combined."

Aegis sucked in a breath but nodded. Nexora was a leader in security hardware and software. "I trust there's a way in for me in this data?"

He nodded. "They're doing new construction. Security is lax there, but there are tunnels that lead into the main building."

That was enough. She palmed the drive, but then hesitated.

"Why are you willing to tell me all this?"

"Because I already made the mistake of telling Nexora no. And because whatever PanOptic is becoming, it scares me more than they do." He leaned back, scrubbing his face with the back of his hand. "They're launching it tomorrow. Full demonstration. Government contracts already lined up. Once it goes live, there's no pulling it back."

She knew most of that already, but it was a good reminder. Aegis rose.

"Whatever you're planning," the informant said, "don't hesitate. Nexora won't."

She paused just long enough to nod, then pushed back into the daylight. Outside, the city hummed, unaware of what was going to happen tonight. They didn't know. But they would soon.

Aegis was going to do her best to save the day.

Claire Sterling tried to shake her hands. They always cramped up right before a mission. She knew why; ever since she was a little kid, she always twisted her fingers and cracked her knuckles when she was nervous. The cramps were merely the memories of so many anxious moments, especially from the time when she discovered her powers and realized what they made possible for her.

She could be a hero, the kind she had always needed.

If she was going to accomplish that lofty goal, she had to focus. She had been planning this infiltration for weeks, and this was her chance. She was finally going to get the answers she sought.

She took a few deep breaths to calm her roiling stomach, leaning forward to peer out the windshield at her target. Nexora's building shone in the night like a beautifully wrapped Christmas present, just waiting for her to open it. She ran her hands down her blouse, making sure the fabric was still smooth. Her fingers snagged on the ID hanging from a lanyard around her neck. That had been the hardest part of her disguise to acquire. She had stalked a Nexora employee for two weeks before she snagged her security credentials. That happened two hours earlier, giving her a narrow window of opportunity.

With one final deep breath, Claire approached Nexora's parking entrance. The guard manning the gate waved her forward when she flashed the ID at him, allowing her to pull up to the security scanner. Her heart fluttered as she pulled up to the sleek silver pillar.

"Please tap ID." The computer's voice was way too cheery for this late at night.

Claire gritted her teeth, trying to keep her fingers from trembling, as she leaned out of the car and did as instructed.

The pillar made a chittering sound, as if it was chewing through the data embedded in the card. Then it prompted, "Please look in the camera for biometric verification."

Once again, Claire followed the command, but as she did, she reached her left hand underneath the camera. Just as the camera lit up, Claire made a fist, her knuckles resting right under the lens. A brilliant foot-long blade of white light burst into existence, erupting from the back of her hand, but that was enough to obscure the camera's view. A second later, she relaxed her hand, and the blade vanished.

Claire sucked in an anxious breath. This trick normally worked. The flash of her blades forming could usually confuse security cameras and facial recognition programs. The timing had to be perfect, but she had plenty of practice. But Nexora's security systems were supposed to be next level. She cast a nervous glance over her shoulder at the guard shack. If this didn't work, the guard would come running, and she'd either have to drive like crazy or fight her way free...

The silver pillar beeped, a friendly little trill, and the voice said, "Welcome back, Lucinda Paulson."

The security arm in front of her swung open. Claire released her held breath, shifted the car into gear, and rolled through, one step closer to her goal.

The lot was mostly empty, meaning she could park close to the entrance. After grabbing the messenger bag she had bought in a thrift shop earlier in the day, she hastened to the main entrance, trying not to hurry. Claire rehearsed her excuse for coming to Nexora so late at night. "Remember: you forgot your earbuds when you left earlier today. Just stopping in to get them and then you're out of here…"

She had to swipe the stolen ID on another card reader to unlock the glass doors. She crossed the lobby, trying not to gawk at the tree growing in the atrium or the three-story tall water feature to her right. Across the lobby was the final checkpoint, manned by a bored-looking security guard. She straightened up, mustering her confidence. Everyone always said she looked much older than her actual age of seventeen, and she had taken the time to style her blond hair and highlight her blue eyes in a way that she hoped would look adult and professional. If she was lucky, the security guard would be fooled into thinking she was an adult.

The guard barely glanced up at her as she approached.

Forcing a smile onto her face, she held out the ID. "Hey! Sorry to bother you. I just forgot my earbuds when I left work earlier, and—"

With a grunt, the guard took the card and swiped it over another reader. When the light next to the reader turned green, he hit a button on the desk, and the security gate next to him swung open. He didn't even look up from his phone.

Claire almost rattled off the rest of her explanation, but she caught herself. Instead, she took the ID, tucked it into her pocket, and hurried through the gate.

Instead of heading toward the elevator, Claire veered off for the nearest restroom. Once inside, she locked the door and ripped open the bag. She shucked her disguise and put on her uniform, starting with the charcoal-gray bodysuit with the reflective material running down her arms and the sides of her legs. Then she slipped on the silver half-jacket, making sure the metallic shoulder pieces stayed in place. The last thing she pulled on was a pair of wide-lensed goggles. She looked in the mirror, checking to make sure she looked okay. Hopefully, no one would see her, but if they did, she wanted to make sure that they'd be impressed.

A tingling sensation washed over her from her head to her toes. She didn't know exactly what caused it whenever she suited up, whether it was nervous energy or something to do with her power. She recognized it for what it was. Claire Sterling had been set aside. Radiant stood in her place.

With a nod to the mirror, Radiant hopped up on the toilet so she could get access to the crawl space above the ceiling. She tapped the sheetrock, then formed one of her blades and cut a hole in the material large enough for her to shimmy through. Once in the ceiling, she headed deeper into the building. Time to find Project PanOptic. Time to find her answers.

Time to find out who killed her mother.

True to the informant's word, the new construction at Nexora's campus was poorly guarded. Aegis had watched the security patrols, timing them out. As near as she could tell, the guards only checked the perimeter every ten minutes. And she hadn't spotted any cameras or other security measures.

All too easy. And that worried her.

Still, she couldn't overlook such a golden opportunity. After another patrol passed her hiding place in the woods surrounding the campus, Aegis waited for an additional five minutes, then crept out of her cover and sprinted toward the construction site. At first, she worried that she would have to cut through the fence that surrounded it, but she found a gap she could shimmy through.

Once she was past that obstacle, she headed for the nearest half-finished building. According to the informant's data, this would eventually become a new R&D facility. Now, though, it looked more like a rotten ribcage, girders jutting up into the darkening sky. All she had to do was make her way toward the tunnels connecting it to the main campus and—

"Hey!" A voice shattered the quiet.

Aegis whirled. A security guard charged at her, pointing and yelling. She winced. How had she not noticed him? Stupid, stupid, stupid!

The guard fumbled at his belt for a weapon. So much for the stealth option. Aegis clenched her fists, triggering her powers. She grunted as a tightness swirled up through her body, from her feet to the top of her head. Her body swelled, and she grew slightly larger as organic armor plates formed just underneath her skin.

To his credit, the guard didn't even flinch at her transformation. He drew his weapon—thankfully, it was just a taser—and fired.

The barbs bounced off Aegis's chest, unable to penetrate her skin. The guard tossed aside the firing mechanism and drew a club. With a battle cry, he swung the weapon and cracked it against the side of her head.

The club snapped in half. The guard finally seemed surprised, backing away from her with wide eyes.

"Sorry." Aegis winced. She hated the way her voice sounded after she transformed, so gravely and low.

The man mouthed a few silent words, but before he could actually say anything, Aegis backhanded him. He spun around from the impact and collapsed to the ground.

Aegis kneeled down and checked his pulse. She didn't think she hit him hard enough to seriously injure him, but she couldn't always be sure. Thankfully, his pulse was still strong.

She rose and rolled her shoulders, grunting at the new stiffness in her joints. Her armor wouldn't get absorbed back into her body for a few hours, depending on how thick it was. Her power was a mixed blessing. Yes, her armor plating was extremely durable. If it grew thick enough, it made her nearly indestructible, but it limited her flexibility. Plus, she didn't like the way it made her look, especially around her head. The thick plating made her look too much like *him*.

She dragged the guard away from where they had fought and stashed him in an out-of-the-way spot where his fellow guards might not find him. Then she headed further into the construction site to find the tunnel that would take her to PanOptic.

It didn't take her long. She squeezed into the opening and shimmied her way through the darkness. A short while later, Aegis grunted as the tunnel walls scraped her arms. Maybe using these access tunnels wasn't such a great idea, especially with her armor. This was a much tighter fit than she had expected. The last thing she wanted to happen was for her to get stuck.

Thankfully, after what felt like hours of crawling, she emerged into the main plant room. As she pulled herself out of the narrow opening, she cast a nervous look around the darkened space. There, to her left, were the furnaces. To her right, pipes and conduits as thick as her waist snaked up into the ceiling. The air thrummed with noise, and the room was hot enough that sweat beaded across her forehead.

She nodded to herself. So far, so good. She had made it inside. Now, to find the main lab and shut down Project PanOptic.

*Ah,* mija. *How good you are to me...*

Aegis winced. She scowled to herself. She wasn't doing this for him. Never for him. Try as she might, though, she couldn't shake the nagging guilt. While she wasn't doing it for him, he would benefit. She would too, at least tangentially. But she reminded herself she was actually doing this for larger, nobler reasons. Squaring her shoulders, she headed for the nearest exit.

Much to her relief, the plant room was deserted. That surprised her. Shouldn't there be a maintenance worker monitoring the systems? Nexora's research and development labs probably needed very specific environmental conditions. This close to the official launch of their flagship product, wouldn't they want to make sure everything was just-so? Their negligence worked to her advantage, though, so she probably shouldn't complain.

After a few minutes of searching, she found a door that led to a stairwell. Aegis crept up the stairs, scanning for security measures. There had to be some.

Nexora was the industry standard for security. Why wouldn't they use it in their own headquarters?

Sure enough, as she approached the first landing, she spotted a tiny white dome nestled in a corner, so small and unobtrusive that she almost didn't notice it. She paused, pulling back, hoping the device hadn't spotted her yet. Aegis waited, counting to fifteen, waiting to see if she could hear the pounding of feet or the angry shouts that would indicate security was on its way. The only sound she heard was the mechanical whirring of the plant room. Good. Time to see if the next step in her plan would work.

She fished a tiny, metallic ball out of a pocket on her belt. She rolled it around in her palm, studying it. A ring of blue lights glowed softly around its center, with a single button on top. According to what she had been told, all she'd need to do was press the button and the device would generate a field that would cloak her from the building's surveillance systems. There was no question in her mind whether it would work; she had stolen it from *him*, after all, and he had used it plenty of times in his career. No, the problem was that using this device, even if she was doing so with good intentions, would be another step in his direction, a trajectory he had always thought her life would take. His was an inevitable gravity, always threatening to pull her down if she let it.

Aegis had to pause, leaning up against the wall, as her breathing became ragged. She pressed a hand to her chest, trying to calm her spasming heart, as she squeezed her eyes shut. Could she do this? Could she really go through with this? Aegis had come to Nexora for all the right reasons. But would using this device taint her attempt?

No, she couldn't panic. She couldn't second-guess herself. Nexora had to be stopped. They couldn't bring Project PanOptic online, and Aegis was going to make sure they wouldn't. If that meant she had to cross this line, she'd have to suck it up.

With a sharp nod, she pressed the button. The blue lights brightened, dancing and flickering before most of the lights disappeared. The few that were left seemed to crawl along. Aegis sucked in a breath. That supposedly meant the device was working. Only one way to find out for sure.

Holding her breath, Aegis climbed up the stairs to the landing. Her gaze was locked onto the dome. There was no way to tell if it had noticed her or not. Its glassy eye merely stared in her direction. Once she reached the landing, she stepped directly under the device and waited, straining her ears to see if there was any indication that she had been detected.

A minute dragged by. Two. Still nothing. Aegis blew out a shaky breath, then pocketed the sphere. She chided herself for being so scared. If she was really going to be a hero, she knew she couldn't hide in a stairwell. She had to keep moving, confront the evil head-on. She had to make a difference. She had to *be* different.

She needed to prove that she wouldn't turn out like her dad.

Radiant was so lost.

When she had come up with this plan, she had figured it would be easy. The hardest part would be sneaking into the building, right? And she knew she could bluff her way in. Bat her eyelashes, put on her best innocent face. Easy as anything. And finding the lab would be even easier. At least it should have been. All roads lead to Rome, so all the halls should have led to the lab. After she dropped out of the ceiling deeper in Nexora's building, she figured it would be so simple to find what she was looking for. She had even crept up to the second floor, and she still hadn't found anything.

"Hey!" a voice shouted. "What are you doing here?"

Radiant snapped around in time to see a security guard in full riot gear charging her. He had pulled a collapsible baton from his belt, whipping it toward the floor to extend it to its full length. A brief burst of panic sliced through her, but she shoved it aside just as quickly. She could handle one guard.

With a roar, the man lifted the baton over his head. Radiant dropped back a step, raising her arms in a defensive stance. Then she squeezed her fists, summoning two lightblades. The shimmering white energy burst from her knuckles on each hand, jutting out a full foot.

To his credit, the guard didn't even flinch. He swung his club at her head, a downward slash that might have fractured her skull.

If it had connected, that is. In one smooth motion, Radiant dropped back another step and swept her right blade up, slicing through the baton. The guard followed through on his swing, but the motion threw him off balance. Radiant stepped forward, using her blades to slice through the straps on the man's tactical vest. The two halves fell open, almost like a flower blossoming. Then Radiant spun out of his way, allowing the momentum of his swing to carry him forward. She stuck a foot in his path, tripping him.

He slammed face-first into the floor, skidding several feet down the hall. Before he could recover, Radiant charged him and kicked him across the head, knocking him out cold.

She tensed, waiting for the guard's partner to investigate. No one came. She breathed out a sigh of relief, then kneeled down to check what the man was carrying. She confiscated his radio and his keycard. She used his own cuffs to bind his hands behind his back, then stashed him in a nearby office.

Radiant held up the keycard and smirked. At least she had a way into the lab now...if she could ever find it.

Aegis eased the door open a crack and peeked through to the empty hallway beyond. She had made it up three flights of stairs and hadn't heard so much as a peep from security. The silence was unnerving more than comforting. Yes, her father's stolen tech had rendered her undetectable to the security systems, but it wouldn't have worked on any guards she might have encountered. Only she hadn't seen any. Where was everyone? The night before Nexora's big debut, and the hallways and stairwells seemed deserted.

Well, she shouldn't pass up the opportunity. The main R&D lab should be just down this hallway. With a nod, she stepped out of the stairwell and crept down the hallway. She just had to make it to the next junction, turn right, and—

There it was! The doors to the lab appeared to be made of thick metal with large glass cutouts. Aegis jogged down the hall, skidding to a stop, her eyes scanning for a button or a knob or a lever to get the door open.

Her gaze landed on a biometric lock, and a shiver rippled over her body. How was she going to get past that? Maybe the stolen tech? She fished the little ball out of her pocket and pressed it against the lock. She wasn't all that surprised when nothing happened, but she was a little disappointed.

"Probably would have been too easy," she muttered to herself.

What were her options? She could encase her hand in thick armor and try punching through the door. Aegis had always been stronger than most average people, a power she had inherited from her father. But would that help here? The door looked much too thick. Her father might have been able to batter his way in—and he would, without any hesitation—but she doubted she could.

Aegis returned to examine the lock. As near as she could tell, there were scanners for fingerprints, retinas, a card reader, and a number pad. She frowned. Did that mean she'd need to pass all four to get through the door? Most likely. Nexora wouldn't want just anyone to waltz in. So how would she get in? Was there another door? Possibly, but it would take time to find it. Even if she could, she doubted there would be lighter security elsewhere.

Returning to the door, she popped up on her toes to peek through one of the glass insets. The window warped her view, but she could just barely glimpse counters, workstations, and... She frowned, adjusting her view to bring the blurry mass in one corner into focus. Were those pipes? Looked like it: thick pipes dropping from the ceiling and snaking...somewhere. Try as she might, she couldn't see where they went.

Then her eyes widened. Maybe she wouldn't be able to get through the door, but maybe she could get in through the ceiling. All she had to do was—

"What do you think you're doing?"

Aegis froze at the question. She wasn't surprised someone had found her. Frankly, she thought that she would have been spotted much sooner. No, the problem was the voice itself. She knew that voice and recognized the speaker.

She groaned and turned around. "What are you doing here?"

Sure enough, Radiant glared at her, her arms crossed. "I asked you first, wrecking ball. What do you think you're doing?"

Aegis returned the expression, trying to inject some heat into it. She should have expected this. Whenever she tried to make any headway in her career, Radiant was right there to mess things up. "I'm here because of Project PanOptic."

Radiant's expression faltered, then softened. "Well, all right then. Glad we're on the same page for once." She held up a keycard. "This might get us inside. If not, we'll figure a way in. Are you okay if I use the system first?"

"What do you mean, 'use it first'?" Aegis frowned. "I'm here to destroy it."

Her eyes flashing, Radiant stammered, then growled. "No, you're not. I need it. I need to find out... to unmask Razorback."

Cold twisted in Aegis's gut, and her mouth went dry. A momentary wave of panic crashed over her. "Wh-why? Why him?"

Radiant scowled at her. "I have my reasons."

They stared at each other, and Aegis noticed that Radiant shifted her weight so that she leaned closer to the door, as if she was getting ready to make a run for it.

"I can't let you do that," Aegis said, stepping between Radiant and the lab door.

"Why not?"

"Because...because..." Her voice trailed off, her mind scrambling for any reason. "Because this technology is dangerous."

"Unmasking supervillains is dangerous? Unmasking terrorists is dangerous?" Radiant countered, her eyes flashing.

"Unmasking superheroes is safe? Unmasking protesters is acceptable?" Aegis countered quietly.

"That would never happen!" Radiant countered, her tone acidic. "Dr. Holloway said so himself. The point of PanOptic is to combat criminals and make sure they can't hide!"

Aegis nodded. She had heard the same claims as well. "But there's no guarantee that the tech will only be used that way. What happens if a bad actor gets it? They'd be able to identify all of us. No one would be safe."

Radiant's cheeks turned bright red. She clenched her fists, and sparkles of light danced across her knuckles. Aegis tensed, but Radiant's blades didn't form.

"Well, what do you think you could do to stop this anyway?" Radiant's voice was almost petulant. "Even if you destroy the prototype, Nexora will just build another one."

Aegis shook her head. "I got some inside information. PanOptic relies on a proprietary device, one of a kind and next to impossible to replace. If I destroy that, they'll be set back for years. Decades, maybe."

Radiant's eyes widened, and a desperate look flashed through them. Aegis tried to keep a calm expression. She really couldn't afford this delay, not when she was so close.

"Look, I don't care what you do to PanOptic after I'm done using it," Radiant finally said. "Use it yourself, destroy it, steal it, it doesn't matter to me. But I need to find out who Razorback is. Now get out of my way."

Stepping between Radiant and the door, Aegis held up a hand. "No. I can't let you do that. I won't let you."

"You won't 'let' me?" Radiant took a step forward, her eyes dark. "I'm not asking for your permission. And I definitely don't need it. Move."

Aegis crossed her arms. As she did, she summoned more of her armor. Her shoulders widened, her arms thickened, and a bony helmet formed around her head. "No."

Radiant took a step back, her gaze sweeping up and down Aegis. "So it's going to be like that?"

"Doesn't have to be," Aegis replied.

For a split second, it looked like Radiant was going to back off. She took another step back, but then she clenched her hands into fists and her brilliant lightblades formed. With a roar, she leaped at Aegis, slashing at her.

Aegis raised her forearms, blocking the attack. In spite of her armor, though, a sizzle of pain ripped into her arms. She hissed, stumbling back a step. Apparently her armor wasn't quite thick enough. She summoned a little more, but not too much. She was already feeling stiff and sluggish as it was; she'd need to stay agile if she was going to take on Radiant. She lashed out, trying to sweep Radiant's legs, but the other hero dodged back, then came in swinging, slicing at her chest and arms again. This time, the lightblades skittered across her armor but couldn't penetrate it.

A frustrated look darted across Radiant's face, but one of determination quickly chased it away. She burst forward, sprinting toward Aegis, her blades extended. Without thinking, Aegis snared her by the shoulders and tossed her over her hip.

Radiant sailed through the air and slammed into the lab's doors. No, she actually slammed *through* the doors, the metal tearing like tinfoil.

Aegis's stomach twisted at the sight. She hadn't meant to throw her that hard!

Aegis stepped up to the door and touched the bent material. She frowned. It was surprisingly flexible. She could actually bend the shards with her bare hands. And it appeared as if the door had been hollow as well, almost as if it was designed to be easy to break through. Rather than puzzle over that oddity, Aegis pushed her way through the hole Radiant's body had created, stepping into the lab beyond.

The room was filled with cables, pipes, and control panels. Aegis ignored all of that, stepping up to Radiant's prone form. The other girl lay in a heap, her arms and legs tangled together. With a gasp, Aegis kneeled down next to her, gingerly trying to feel for a pulse, but her fingers were encased in armor, thick and clumsy. She couldn't feel anything. Maybe she'd be able to feel her breath against her cheek. She leaned in closer to see...

With a cry, Radiant swung at her, a lightblade forming at her knuckles. A brilliant light tore through Aegis's vision, the world suddenly awash in prickling pain and starbursts. She fell backward, clawing at her eyes and screeching. She was blind! Radiant had sliced her through her eyes. She swung a fist in the other girl's direction but didn't connect with her. She could hear Radiant scrambling away from her.

Aegis snarled. She hadn't wanted to fight the other hero, but now she didn't have a choice. Radiant may have escalated matters, but Aegis was going to put an end to all of this.

Radiant scrabbled away from Aegis, who sat on the floor, rubbing at her eyes. That wouldn't last long, though. The moment Aegis recovered, the fight would restart. If she was going to take advantage of the momentary lull, she'd have to act fast.

She popped to her feet and glanced around the room, frowning. Was this really all there was to the lab? The room was small, twenty by ten, if that. There was a table built into the wall on her left, with three laptops open and running on top of it. There was another door in front of her with a thick collection of pipes and wires snaking from the floor to the ceiling to the right of that. To her right, there were two large flat-screen monitors that displayed readouts of some kind, waving lines and patterns scrolling by. Was PanOptic on one of the laptops? She hurried over to them, her eyes frantically darting across the screens. The first one was open to an email program. The second, technical schematics of some kind. The third... was that a video game? Who leaves a video game running on a work laptop? Radiant's heart fluttered. Was PanOptic a hoax? No, that couldn't be right, given all the fanfare that Nexora had been giving it. The schematics on the second laptop were for Project PanOptic. Was the control interface somewhere on that computer?

The skin on the back of her neck prickled. Danger, looming behind her! She dodged to her right just as Aegis's fist crashed down on the table, nearly ripping it from the wall. With a roar, Aegis whirled and punched at Radiant, who barely had time to duck.

Radiant backpedaled, igniting both of her blades and raising them in a defensive stance. "Okay, now hold on. Let's talk about this." She doubted this would work, but it was worth a shot.

Aegis bellowed and swung again. Radiant barely had time to duck out of the way. The momentum of the swing carried Aegis forward, and she nearly pitched into the massive pipe that ran from floor to ceiling. She whirled and flexed her arms. Somehow, she grew even bigger, her arms, chest, and legs growing thicker and more blocky.

Radiant's eyes widened at the sight. Fire blazed through her body, chased away by icy tendrils. How was she going to stop Aegis now? Her blades hadn't been able to cut through her armor before. Now the other girl was likely unstoppable. There had to be a way to at least slow her down.

Her gaze fell on the light switch next to the door. Would that work? She had little choice. As Aegis took another swing at her, she rolled under her arm, popped up, and slammed a blade into the switch. The lights overhead flickered and then went out. Radiant started to smile, but then she realized that the light from the hall spilled in. The room was dimmer, but not enough to make much of a difference.

"Hold still!" Aegis bellowed, then charged her again.

Radiant tried to dodge again, but she couldn't move quite fast enough. Aegis's outstretched fist clipped her in the side of the head, sending Radiant spinning away. She slammed into the monitors, shattering them. Shaking her head to clear it, she stumbled forward, just as Aegis charged her again. This time, Radiant spun out of the way, slicing at Aegis's knees as she did. Her blades skittered across the other girl's armor, but sank in enough that Aegis shrieked in pain and stumbled—

Charging headlong into the massive pipe in the room's corner. Aegis collided with enough force that the metal cracked, spraying her with a cloudy white gas. Frost crawled across Aegis's skin, and she screamed, swiping at her arms and legs and back. The armor plating under her skin crackled and then shattered, bits and pieces of thick organic plating showering from her limbs. Radiant stared on in horror as Aegis tried to wipe away whatever it was. A sweet smell filled the air, chased by a bitter cold.

Almost immediately, alarms ripped through the air, the hallway outside bathed in rotating red lights. Radiant spun toward the lab's entrance, just in time to see a thick door slam down from the ceiling, trapping them inside. She sputtered and coughed as the gas spraying from the pipe crawled across the floor and crept up her legs. Her lungs burned, and she quickly realized how dangerous this was. How were they going to get out?

Wait, the other door! She jumped over to it and gave it an experimental push. Much to her surprise and relief, it wasn't locked. She shouldered it open, then snared Aegis's hand and pulled the other girl through. Just as they rolled into the room beyond, another thick door slammed into place, trapping them inside.

Radiant stumbled a few steps, then turned to Aegis. The other hero looked horrible. Large sections of her skin appeared to have torn away, leaving angry red welts up and down her arms and legs. She hacked and coughed, but she seemed steady enough. Radiant shuddered, the memory of the cold gas clinging to her. It didn't seem like it could get into this room, whatever it was.

As she stood there, trying to get her bearings, overhead lights snapped on, revealing a room with clinically white walls and floors with chrome accents. A ten-foot tall cylinder filled one side of the room, with tubes and pipes and wires running in and out of it. A control panel sat in front of the cylinder, with a large viewscreen. A logo depicting an open eye rotated on the screen, only to be replaced by a stylized font declaring "PROJECT PANOPTIC."

A thrill raced through Radiant. She had done it. She had found PanOptic. Time to get her answers.

The fire raging across Aegis's skin was finally beginning to subside. She resisted the urge to scrub at the spots on her arms and legs where her armor had shattered. From experience, she knew that doing so would only irritate it further. Thankfully, she knew a trick to deal with the injuries. Taking a deep, stuttering breath, she summoned a thin layer of armor over the welts and sores. Her arms and legs still ached and burned, but the pain was tolerable. When her body naturally absorbed that armor later, she'd be fully healed.

Next, she swiped at her eyes. Ghostly afterimages danced in her vision, the remnants of Radiant's attack on her. At first, she had worried that she had been permanently blinded. Thankfully, that hadn't been the case.

Forcing herself to shake off the lingering aches and pains, she looked around the room Radiant had dragged her into. The first thing she noticed was the cameras in each of the four corners, monitoring whatever happened in this room. Next, her gaze fell on all the different pipes and conduits running into the gleaming silver pillar. She frowned, taking a step closer to them. One thick pipe was labeled "oxygen." Another was labeled "waste." Still another "water." Some of the wire bundles had tags for "monitoring" and "output." She traced their path through the room, noting how they all converged on the large cylinder.

Then Radiant screamed, a frustrated shriek, pounding on the control panel. Aegis crept up behind her, wary of being noticed. She didn't want to restart their fight, especially given how much her whole body ached.

Hunched over the control panel's keyboard, Radiant tried typing something else, but once again, the console blatted at her, warning her about another failed attempt. She kicked the console, then whirled on Aegis. "Do you know the password?"

Aegis quickly shook her head. She didn't, but she also didn't want to make it seem like she did but wasn't sharing it.

Radiant roared incoherently, then turned back to the console. She typed in something else, and the console *blatted* at her, the screen flashing red. Radiant screeched in frustration, making a fist and forming one of her lightblades. She cocked her arm back as if ready to slice into the console.

Without thinking, Aegis darted forward and caught her arm before she could strike. "Whoa, hold on there. Let's not start stabbing things just yet, okay?"

At first, Radiant seemed ready to fight her, but then she sagged in the hold. She shook off Aegis's hand and muttered, "Fine."

Once she was sure that Radiant had calmed down, Aegis turned to the door that had sealed them into this room. She knocked a knuckle against it experimentally. It felt solid and thick, unlike the door she had tossed Radiant through. Worse, she couldn't find any way to open it. No switches, levers, emergency releases, nothing. Aegis considered punching the door out of frustration, but after stopping Radiant from attacking the console, she figured that would be kind of hypocritical.

The console *blatted* again, and Radiant bit off a curse. Aegis turned back to her. The other girl appeared calmer, but she was back at the keyboard, trying to break the password again. Aegis sighed and stepped up to her.

"Don't try to stop me," Radiant said, her voice a warning growl.

Aegis almost pointed out that she didn't need to do anything since Radiant didn't know the password, but she didn't. Best not to antagonize her. But then Radiant's shoulders started shuddering, almost as if she was laughing. Aegis took a step closer and realized that no, she wasn't laughing. She was crying. Tears streamed down her cheeks, and she was quietly sobbing.

"Hey, settle down. It's going to be okay." She tried to place a comforting hand on Radiant's shoulder.

Radiant shrugged her hand off and whirled on her. "What do you know about this? I have to find out who killed my mother! I've been waiting ten years to find out. I can't give up, not when I'm so close. I have to use PanOptic. It's the only way I'll ever find out who Razorback actually is!"

A twinge tugged at Aegis's chest. She pursed her lips as if trying to clamp her mouth shut. *Good girl*, mija. *Protect your family.* Her father's voice, an echo of what he probably would have said in this situation.

Should she tell her? The weight of her knowledge pressed down on her, heavy enough that she almost broke. But no, she couldn't.

Instead, she prompted, "What happened?"

"When I was six, my mom went on a business trip to Dallas. No big deal, she went on those all the time." Radiant turned to look at Aegis, her eyes hollow, her expression blank. "The first few days, she called in every night to wish me a goodnight and sing me..." She swiped more tears from her eyes. "But then she stopped calling. Dad tried to play it off like it was no big deal; she was too busy, but I could tell he was worried.

"And then, at school, I heard something about how some super-powered individuals got into a fight in Dallas. Lots of damage to the downtown area, lots of people hurt and killed. When I got home, I asked Dad if Mom had been there when it happened. The color just drained from his face, and that's when I knew. I knew what he was trying to hide from me."

Aegis's stomach twisted, and sweat prickled her brow. Maybe she shouldn't have asked. That weight she carried felt even heavier.

Radiant didn't seem to notice her discomfort. "I found out years later what happened. In the middle of the fight, Razorback threw a truck into a hotel lobby, the same one where Mom was staying. Killed five people and injured fifteen others. Mom was one of the five. A few years later, my powers manifested for the first time, and I knew. I knew why I could do this." She squeezed a fist, forming one of her lightblades. "I was going to find out who Razorback was, and I'm going to make him regret killing my mom."

Silence descended on the room, although Aegis thought she heard her father's distant mocking laughter. She was vaguely aware of blaring sirens in the distance. Why hadn't anyone come to investigate what had happened yet?

When it became clear that Radiant was done with her story, Aegis ventured a question. "Didn't Razorback...disappear like three years ago?"

Radiant snorted. "That's what everyone says, but I know he's still out there. He's probably gone into hiding. But with PanOptic, I'll finally find out who he is. I'll find him, and I'll make sure he faces justice."

Aegis nodded, but in the back of her mind, she heard her father's chuckle. *How well you take care of me*, mija. She winced, screwing her eyes shut. It would be so easy, just let the truth slip from her mouth, just put an end to all of this...

"How are your eyes?" Radiant asked quietly.

Surprise rippled through Aegis, and she said, "Better."

"Good." Radiant tapped a fist against her thigh. "I'm sorry I did that. You weren't in any danger of losing your sight. I can control the intensity of my blades. When I sliced you, I was just trying to temporarily blind you. Sorry."

Aegis shrugged. "I didn't really give you much choice, did I?"

Radiant chuckled. "I guess not."

They stared at each other, an uneasy tension between them.

Finally, Aegis took a shuddering breath, then said, "You can't get anything from that console?"

Radiant turned back to the keyboard. "Not really. I can call up a schematic for this device, but I can't get to the actual interface that would allow me to find out who Razorback really is. Look!"

Aegis stepped up behind Radiant and peeked over her shoulder. The other girl backed out of the password prompt to the main menu. She poked the screen, selecting "Schematics." A new screen appeared, a flurry of lines and connections between different components, showing how everything in PanOptic was connected to each other. Aegis didn't understand anything she saw. Most of it was labeled with technical jargon that made little sense to her. She thought she spotted six different computer processors, plus dozens of other connected systems. She blinked several times, a small ache twisting behind her eyes.

But then she frowned. All the lines, all the connections, seemed to converge in something merely labeled as the "Prime Component." She gently moved Radiant aside so she could take control of the readout. She scrolled around the schematic, confirming her suspicions. Everything came together in that one spot.

"What do you suppose that 'Prime Component' is?" Radiant asked.

Aegis frowned and leaned in closer. "I don't know. Looks like it's the heart of PanOptic, whatever it is. I think it's in that cylinder there."

Radiant suddenly gasped. She nudged Aegis out of the way and started calling up submenus, finally selecting one labeled "MAINTENANCE."

"What are you doing?" Aegis asked.

"Maybe if we can get physical access to that Prime Component, maybe I can bypass the security and get some answers," Radiant said. "Or maybe I can remove it and find someone who can hack into it."

Aegis's frown deepened. Removing whatever it was didn't seem like a smart idea. So many pipes and wires and tubes went into that cylinder. Her gaze roamed over what she could see in the room. The oxygen line, a pipe for water, another for waste. And still another for...

Her eyes widened when she spotted it: a thin pipe labeled "nutrients."

"Radiant, I think that..." she started to say.

There was a loud crack, and the control panel slid to the right. The cylinder rumbled toward them, tipping backward as it moved. Aegis and Radiant dodged out of the way as it came to rest between them. The cylinder hissed, and a seam appeared across its top, running lengthwise. Two panels rose an inch, then split down the middle. They slid down the cylinder's sides, and a white mist bubbled out of the opening, spilling down to the floor and creeping towards them. Aegis stumbled back a step, gagging on the overly sweet smell.

Radiant stepped forward, waving away the vapor, and peeked inside. Her eyes went wide, and she bit off a curse.

Aegis approached the cylinder as well, bracing herself even though she suspected she knew what she'd see.

Inside the cylinder was a small chamber, one lined with dingy white cushions. And resting on the cushions was an unconscious person. She appeared to be in her late twenties, but that was hard to judge with any accuracy. She wore a white jumpsuit that probably should have hugged her body, but she was so gaunt the material hung loosely around her. Her head was shaved, probably to allow for the many wires and electrodes that pierced her skin. Tubes ran in and out of her mouth and her nose, and others snaked out of ports in her clothing. The woman moaned softly, and her body twitched, but she didn't give any other indication that she was aware of what was happening to her.

"What is going on?" Radiant whispered.

A heavy weight settled in Aegis's stomach. "I think she is the Prime Component. I think this is how PanOptic works."

Radiant stared at the woman, her eyes wide. Was Aegis right? Was the Prime Component a person? No, that didn't make sense! In all of Nexora's press releases, Dr. Holloway said that PanOptic was just really advanced facial recognition software. But if that were true, why was this woman hooked into the system?

"I don't think you're going to be able to hack her," Aegis said, her voice quiet.

With a snarl, Radiant shot a glare at the other girl, who stood on the other side of the cylinder. She couldn't argue the point, though. If the Prime Component had been some sort of computer thingamabob, she could have removed it, taken it out of the building, and found someone who could hack into it. But looking at all the tubes and wires connected to this woman, she couldn't just disconnect her. That could kill her!

"Do you think she volunteered for this?" Aegis asked.

That was a good question, too. As much as Radiant wanted to believe that the woman had, looking at her again made her think the opposite was the case. "I don't think so."

Radiant leaned in to take a closer look. The woman, whoever she was, might have been pretty at one point, but now she looked fragile. Radiant was reminded of how her grandmother looked right before she died of cancer not that long ago. She had been so much older than this woman, though. Or was that the case? Radiant honestly couldn't tell. The woman lying in the cylinder could have been in her thirties or her sixties.

"What are you going to do now?" Aegis asked, her voice quiet.

Heat flashed through Radiant. She glared at Aegis and snapped, "I don't know, okay? The better question is, what are you going to do? You said you were going to destroy PanOptic. Still planning on doing that? You gonna kill this lady?"

Aegis blanched, the exposed parts of her face turning pale. She looked down, not willing to meet her glare, which Radiant took as a minor victory.

"No, I'm not," Aegis whispered. "But that just begs the question: what are we going to do? What can we do?"

That was the better question. What could they do? Radiant pressed her hands on the edge of the cylinder, then blew out a long breath, trying to sort through the options.

Should they try to remove the woman from the cylinder? That didn't seem like a wise idea, given the sheer number of tubes and wires connecting her to the rest of the system. She didn't feel like they should leave her in Nexora either. Something deep inside her said that this was wrong, that if this woman really was the heart of PanOptic, the company would have said something about it. That they hadn't implied they were trying to hide her participation. Maybe they could take pictures of everything, release them to the public, and expose Nexora? No, that probably wouldn't work. The company probably had an expensive PR team and lawyers who would spin the story and bury it. No, they had to do something, and they had to do it now.

"We need to get her out of here." Hesitation bled through her voice at first, but that quickly evaporated as she stared at the woman. "I don't care how we do it. We can't leave her here."

Aegis nodded, but then asked, "How are we going to do that? Don't forget, we're trapped in here."

"Details." Radiant waved a hand like she was shooing away a pesky insect. "Let's take it one step at a time. How do we get her free from all the life support?"

"You could just...you know, cut everything." Aegis's voice was hesitant. "She might go into shock or something, but if we can get her out of Nexora fast enough, we could get her to a hospital, and they might help."

Radiant shook her head. "Too many ifs and maybes."

Aegis blew out a long breath. "Let's look at the computer again. Maybe it'll have some instructions or something."

That was as good an idea as anything. Radiant moved over to the control panel. She had to return to the main screen, and for just a second, she was tempted to break the password one last time. If they disconnected the woman, she knew her chance would be gone. But then she pursed her lips and called up the sub-menus.

"For what it's worth, I'm sorry about your mom," Aegis said quietly.

Radiant's eyes burned, and she swiped at them. She would not cry. Not in front of Aegis. She would not humiliate herself like that. Besides, she couldn't afford to get distracted. She shrugged one shoulder and said, "It's fine. This is just a setback. I'm going to find out who Razorback is eventually. And then I'm going to make sure that he pays for what he did."

She turned back to the computer, but she noticed Aegis staring at her. Finally, she looked up and met her gaze.

Aegis hesitated, then said, "Radiant...Razorback is dead. He died three years ago."

Numbness swept through her. She took a step closer to her. "That's not true. If Razorback was dead, I'd know. There would have been news reports, some sort of announcement." Tears stung her eyes. "Detective Hu promised he would keep me updated on the case. If Razorback had been killed, he would have told me."

"He probably doesn't know." Aegis's voice had become a whisper. "The authorities...they covered it up. Made it look like an accident, hid his real identity from everyone."

Radiant gaped at Aegis. "What? Why?" But then a more important question blazed within her. "How do you know this?"

Aegis closed her eyes and clenched her jaw, like she was trying to hold back the words. But then her shoulders slumped. "Because I was there when it happened," she whispered.

She *what*? Ice sluiced through Radiant's veins.

"What?" Radiant whispered. "Why would you have been there?"

Aegis sucked in a long, shuddering breath, then looked Radiant square in the eye. "Because Razorback was my father."

Time seemed to freeze. The admission hung in the air between them. And then Radiant clenched her fists, summoning her lightblades.

Aegis took a step backward, raising her hands. As she did, she summoned more armor. Her arms, legs, and chest thickened. She hoped it wouldn't come to blows, but given the way Radiant stared at her, her expression cold, her lightblades glowing brightly from her knuckles, she suspected they would fight.

"He was what?" Radiant whispered, taking a step toward Aegis.

She swallowed hard, but she forced herself to speak. "He's...he was my father. Razorback was. It's true." She winced at the fear lacing through her words. "I was there when he died. My whole family was. We...we were pleading with him to surrender, but he just wouldn't and then..."

"Why would they cover it up?" Radiant asked, her voice ice.

"Because...because of my *abuelo*. My grandfather. He is...was a superhero. The Dallas Dillo. *Abuelo* used his contacts in the government to cover up what happened." Her gaze dropped to the floor. "He didn't want anyone to know about the family connection. He didn't want them to know I'm his daughter."

As Radiant stared at her, Aegis could feel more than just the other girl's gaze. For a moment, it felt like her father was glaring at her as well, chiding her for sharing his secret. A shudder passed through her. She had been carrying this secret with her for so long. Even though she suspected Radiant was about to attack her, she felt better. Lighter. Freer.

Radiant's gaze swept over her, and she laughed. "I should have seen it right away. You and your father inherited your grandfather's power, didn't you?"

Aegis nodded. "Only my father figured out how to grow spikes and blades from his armor."

The other girl snarled, and Aegis regretted having said that. They both knew full well how her father had used those blades.

Radiant took another step closer. "Why didn't you tell me before, when I told you why I was here?"

Many excuses tumbled through her mind. Because Radiant didn't actually need to know. Because she wanted to keep her family issues private. Because *abuelo* would be so disappointed to know she had told someone. Ultimately, though, she shared the truth.

"Because I was scared," she whispered. "I was scared about what would happen if my secret was revealed. I was scared that people would make the connection and realize who I was. I was scared I would lose my friends if they knew what a monster my dad was." She gestured toward Radiant's lightblades. "I was scared that other heroes wouldn't trust me, that I'd never be given the opportunity to make up for all the evil things he did."

Radiant's eyes narrowed, and Aegis sucked in a breath, holding it. She braced herself for what she knew was coming. They were going to fight again. She glanced around the room. Maybe she could steer the brawl toward the far corner, away from the cylinder. The last thing she wanted to happen was for the mystery woman to get injured.

But Radiant's hands relaxed and her lightblades winked out. "I think I understand," she whispered. She glanced over at the cylinder. "Is that why you wanted to destroy PanOptic? To protect yourself? To protect him?"

Aegis considered lying, but then decided against it. "Partially. But it's not just that. My *abuelo* has a saying: 'Never create a weapon you wouldn't want your worst enemy to have.' I think that's the problem here. Could you imagine what would happen if someone like my father got his hands on PanOptic?"

Radiant turned and stared at the cylinder. Then she said quietly, "I hadn't thought of it like that." She nodded. "Then let's get this woman out of here."

With a nod, Aegis leaned in to look at the control panel, scanning the sub-menus. Her gaze hitched on one. "What's this? 'Transport mode'?"

Radiant called up the menu, and then she laughed. "If I'm understanding this right, this will close up the cylinder and disconnect it from the PanOptic system. There are even some wheels that will pop out of the bottom for easy movement."

Aegis frowned. "But won't that hurt the woman?"

"I don't think so." Radiant pointed at the screen. "According to this, there's a temporary life support system that activates, one that would last for two or three hours."

That would be more than enough time for them to get her out of the building. Aegis nodded, but then she realized they had another problem. They were on the second floor of the building, and they were trapped, sealed away behind a thick metal door.

Her gaze drifted toward the floor, and a smile tickled her lips.

"What?" Radiant asked.

"I think I have an idea. Get your blades ready. We're going to have to move fast."

"Are you ready?" Aegis asked.

Radiant shook her hands. No, she wasn't. Not at all. In theory, Aegis's idea was good. But now that they were on the verge of actually doing it, she was terrified she was going to screw this up and badly. They didn't really have any other choices, though. Not if they wanted to get out of the lab. Not if they wanted to save the woman. Not if they wanted to be heroes.

So she nodded, then hunched over the keyboard and activated the cylinder's transport mode. The doors hissed shut, sealing the woman inside again. At first, nothing happened, but then, the tubes and pipes that connected the cylinder to the rest of the device popped away, each time punctuated by a sharp *snap-hiss*. When the last connection broke, the cylinder lifted from the floor, revealing four wheels underneath.

Aegis peeked underneath, then flashed a thumbs up at Radiant. Good. So far, so good. Now all they had to do was—

An alarm klaxon blared, loud enough that Radiant covered her ears by instinct. Aegis didn't seem affected. She waved and shouted, but Radiant couldn't hear what she was saying. Finally, Aegis gestured toward the floor emphatically, and she realized what she wanted. They had to keep acting, in spite of the alarm.

Radiant peeled her hands from her ears. The sound ripped through her head, but she tried to power through the painful disorientation. She ran to the cylinder and summoned her lightblades. She forced herself to make them as strong as she could, much stronger than she usually did. Then she stabbed them into the floor at one corner of the cylinder. She crept along the edge, cutting through the floor, tracing along three sides of the cylinder.

The plan they had come up with was simple: using her blades, Radiant would cut a U-shape around the cylinder, the weight of which would cause the floor to drop. This would form a ramp. Aegis would ride the cylinder down to the first floor to make sure it didn't crash into anything. There were dozens of things that might go wrong, but Radiant hadn't been able to think of a better plan.

She quickly finished the cut, then stepped back, waiting. The floor groaned, and she thought she felt something pop and break through her feet. Radiant held her breath. Aegis, straddling the cylinder, tensed, ready for the fall.

Nothing happened. The floor didn't so much as buckle.

Aegis craned her neck to examine the cut. Then she waved at Radiant and shouted something. Radiant frowned, still unable to hear anything over the blaring siren. She took a step closer and motioned for Aegis to repeat herself. The other girl did.

This time, Radiant barely heard her words over the cacophony: "...too shallow...make...longer?"

It took her a moment to fill in the blanks, but then she understood. Aegis thought she hadn't cut through the floor completely. Could she make her blades any longer to be sure?

Radiant hesitated. Technically, she could. She usually kept her lightblades only a foot long, eighteen inches at the most. She had made them two-and-a-half feet once, but the effort had been overwhelming and she had only maintained them for a few seconds. But what other choice did she have?

She widened her stance, breathing deeply, and then clenched her fists. A growl built in her throat as she imagined the blades springing free, longer than they had ever been before, long enough to cut through the floor entirely. A fire burned across her knuckles, then crept up her forearms. A wordless shout burst from her mouth as she formed her blades, then forced them to grow longer and longer. With each new inch, she screamed louder and louder until, with a burst of energy, the blades extended out four feet. Her shout turned into a shriek. It felt as though her muscles and veins and bones were being extracted through her knuckles. Thankfully, the agony dulled a bit once the blades were fully formed. She nearly collapsed with relief, but she knew she couldn't rest.

Hurrying to the same spot she had started, Radiant plunged the longer blade into the same groove. Although she couldn't be certain, it felt like she had pierced all the way through the floor. She dragged the blade along the same path, hurrying as much as she could. Aegis shouted something, but she couldn't hear it over the alarm and the pounding of her own heart. She made the two corners quickly, then yanked her blade free when she reached the end of the cut. She dismissed the blade, shaking out her hand to get rid of the last vestiges of pain, and waited.

Once again, nothing happened, and Radiant worried they'd have to come up with a different plan. But then, with a loud *crack* she felt through her legs, the cylinder dropped a few inches. She sucked in a breath and held it. Hopefully, the floor would drop, forming the ramp, and—

Instead, the floor dropped out from under the cylinder. Radiant barely registered the surprised look on Aegis's face before she plunged through the hole with the cylinder.

Radiant crept to the hole and peered over the edge. "Aegis!" she shouted. "Are you okay?"

Much to her surprise, she heard the other girl shout back, "I think so. Jump down! I'll catch you!"

She took one more look around the room and then stepped over the edge, plummeting.

With a grunt, she landed in Aegis's outstretched arm. The alarm still blared through the hole, but it wasn't nearly as loud. Radiant took a moment to glance around their surroundings. With a start, she recognized them. This room had been on the tour she had taken of Nexora a few weeks earlier, where they watched a promotional video of Dr. Holloway explaining the benefits of all the wonderful technology Nexora was developing. Now, though, the room was dark and empty save for the cylinder, Aegis, and her.

She blew out a shuddering breath. "All right. So far, so—"

The doors at the far end of the room banged open, light flooding in. Two men in security uniforms charged in, guns drawn. With no sort of warning, they opened fire.

Radiant flinched, but then she realized that Aegis had dodged in front of her. The bullets slammed into the other girl, but she didn't so much as grunt, her body swelling.

"Go!" Aegis grunted.

That was all the prompting Radiant needed. She snapped out her lightblades and darted out from behind her impromptu partner. The guards shouted in surprise, but then Radiant was on them, slicing through the barrels of their guns and kicking their legs out from under them. Then Aegis charged in, her massive fists swinging, knocking the two men out. Within moments, both guards were down and groaning.

"Let's go!" Aegis shouted, heading back to the cylinder.

Thankfully, the fall didn't seem to have damaged the cylinder's wheels. Aegis could get behind and push it out the open doors. Radiant led the way, blades out and ready. Thankfully, there weren't any guards in the hallway. As they approached the main lobby, Radiant sliced through a panel of light switches, plunging the lobby into darkness. The guard at the main desk shouted in surprise, but Radiant quickly disarmed him and knocked him out as Aegis shoved the cylinder across the open area and through the front doors. They emerged into the cool night air, and Aegis steered the rolling mass across the parking lot and into the open field beyond.

Radiant caught up to her just as the cylinder rolled to a stop. Aegis leaned against it, her chest heaving. Radiant nearly slammed into her, but collapsed against the cylinder. She beamed at the other hero, who chuckled in return.

They had done it! They had gotten out of the building with the woman. Now all they had to do was figure out how to get off Nexora's campus and—

She was suddenly aware of someone clapping, a slow, methodical beat. Radiant could almost feel the sarcasm in the staccato rhythm. She whirled around, surprised to see a rail-thin man standing nearby. He was in his mid-twenties, a scruff of brown hair jutting out at insane angles. He wore thick glasses and a rumpled black suit that hung loosely on his frame. He stepped forward, his mouth twitching in a disturbing smile, as he continued his slow applause.

"Is that who I think it is?" Aegis whispered.

Radiant nodded. Dr. Adrian Holloway, the founder and CEO of Nexora. What was he doing here?

He stopped clapping, shoving his hands into his pockets. "I wondered what was taking you so long," he said, his voice a reedy whisper they could barely hear. "By my calculations, you both entered my facility well over an hour ago. But I suppose delays should be expected, given that you are both amateurs."

Heat flashed through Radiant's chest. "Who are you calling an 'amateur'?"

Holloway turned to face her, his eyes flashing. "Why, I'm calling you that, Claire Sterling. And I'm including Marisol Reyes in that assessment as well."

Radiant froze. So did Aegis. They exchanged uncertain looks. Had he just said their secret identities out loud?

He chuckled. "Don't be surprised. PanOptic identified you from various news reports. You are to be commended, although I must admit to some annoyance. I had hoped this bait would attract bigger fish."

"What 'bait?'" Aegis spat.

"Why, the little tendrils of information I've been sending out, hoping people like you would notice. Such as the information broker you consulted, Miss Reyes. Where do you think he got his gossip? Or you, Miss Sterling? Don't you find it unusual that you could procure passes to tour my facilities? Why would a high school student be given such an opportunity?"

Radiant's stomach twisted inside her. It had all been a setup.

Holloway shrugged. "I suppose it doesn't matter. Your participation will suffice."

Aegis took a step forward, and her body swelled even larger. "Suffice for what?"

Holloway grinned, a bare twitch of his lips. "Why, for the narrative I am crafting. Imagine the news reports tomorrow: 'Frantic vigilantes break into Nexora to destroy PanOptic!' 'Dozens dead in vigilante attack!' 'CEO Holloway vows full support and use of PanOptic to stop the vigilante scourge.'"

Radiant frowned. "Dozens dead? We didn't kill anyone!"

"That's not what the news reports will say, not after the authorities discover dozens of my employees dead at their stations from your obvious rampage. Why, their bodies are all strewn through the building right now." He chuckled. "Or they will be in a matter of moments."

Aegis bit off a curse in Spanish. "There'll be no proof we did it."

Holloway quirked a brow at her. "Oh, but there will be. Security footage showing your attack. Forensic evidence of your intrusion. Autopsy reports, showing death from blunt force trauma and slashes from those impressive laser swords of yours."

"They're lightblades!" Radiant countered. When Aegis shot her an incredulous look, she huffed. "Well, they are."

"Regardless, the evidence will be irrefutable. Thankfully, Nexora's state-of-the-art security system could neutralize you both, ensuring that you won't be a threat to anyone else, but the damage will be done," Holloway said. "The government will have no choice but to crack down on superpowered vigilantes. With the help of Nexora and PanOptic, we'll be able to unmask all of them."

Radiant frowned. While all of that sounded horrific, especially given the calm way Holloway described it, her mind hitched on one detail. "What security system? Nothing tried to neutralize us."

Holloway chuckled, removing his glasses. "Quite right, Miss Sterling. Nothing has. At least, not yet."

Then Holloway's body expanded. His arms and legs swelled, then burst open, silvery tentacles spilling out of his appendages. His chest ripped through his suit, his skin turning a sickly metallic color. His head sank into his torso, his face expanding. His mouth twisted into a jagged line, and green light spilled from his eyes. His body continued to grow and writhe as more tentacles spilled out of him, creeping across the open plain.

"You see, Miss Sterling, Miss Reyes, I am the security system." Holloway's voice had taken on a grating, synthetic warble. "And I assure you, I am more than capable of neutralizing you both."

Aegis's heart thundered in her ears. Holloway had completely transformed, turning into what looked like a gigantic metal octopus. He towered over them, at least twenty feet tall, his tentacles spreading across the open area. She gagged on her own bile, suddenly nauseated. While most of his body seemed to have burst, she could still see strips of flesh woven through the metal. A strange grating sound accompanied every movement he made, like steel being drawn over concrete.

"Well, that's horrifying," Radiant muttered. She clenched her fists, her light-blades forming.

"That's not the word I would've chosen," Aegis replied, widening her stance and dropping into a ready position.

With a screech, Holloway charged them, slashing two of his tentacles at them. Radiant dove out of the way. Aegis raised her arms to block the blow. It felt like a semi had hit her, and she could feel the plating in her arms crack under the onslaught. She grunted, but shoved the tentacle aside, thickening the plates in her forearms again.

Radiant darted in, slashing at the tentacle with her blades. But the glowing weapons skittered across the metallic surface without leaving so much as a mark. The other girl's eyes widened, and she bit back a curse, but then the tentacle slapped her away. She tumbled over the ground, landing in a heap of tangled limbs.

Aegis whirled to face Holloway, who loomed over her. With a roar of her own, Aegis charged, dodging another strike. She leaped onto one of the tentacles, clambering up it toward Holloway's face. As she approached, she cocked her arm back and slammed her fist into one of his eyes.

Her knuckles crunched as she made contact and pain blazed up her arm. She bit back a scream and cradled her hand in her other arm. Then a tentacle wrapped around her, plucking her away and tossing her at Radiant. Aegis hit the ground and rolled, coming to rest next to the other girl.

"How...how're we doin'?" Radiant asked, her voice thick. "Winning?"

Aegis coughed, pain lancing through her chest. "I wouldn't... wouldn't call it that."

Radiant grunted and tried to clamber to her feet. "Gonna have to do better then."

Holloway chortled. "Oh, it's much too late for that. While I've enjoyed this minor diversion, I suspect the authorities will be here at any moment. Best to wrap this up, don't you think?"

He whipped one of his tentacles down. Aegis surged to her feet and caught it, but she felt the armor on her arms shatter again. Worse, pain lanced through her legs as the impact drove her an inch into the ground. She grunted, trying to hold the tentacle back.

"Aegis!" Radiant shouted. "Hold on!"

Aegis tried to say something, but she couldn't get the words past the knot in her throat. What could they do? Holloway was clearly too big, too powerful for them to fight on their own. He was going to kill them, and then he would take the woman in the cylinder back into the building. They had lost. They had—

Wait. What was that?

Off in the distance, she could hear a high-pitched whine, one that grew louder and louder with each passing second. After a few moments, Holloway seemed to notice. The tentacle crushing Aegis slackened. It was still heavy, dangerously so, but it didn't seem heavy. She risked a peek. He was looking around as if trying to find the source of the noise.

Then, suddenly, an object rocketed out of the woods. Whatever it was slammed into the side of Holloway's massive head and exploded in a blaze of fire. Holloway screeched, the impact throwing him off balance. The tentacle slipped from Aegis's hands, and she nearly collapsed, additional pains radiating through her hands and arms. What was going on? What happened?

"Look!" Radiant whispered.

Aegis glanced in the direction Radiant pointed and froze. A figure hovered thirty feet in the air, looking down at Holloway. The newcomer wore a bright blue uniform with a rising star logo in the middle of his chest. The golden armor on his shoulders and arms glinted in the dim light. While a mask covered most of his face, his blond hair waved lazily in the wind. Bright green eyes glared down at the massive Holloway, only his lips twisted into a smirk.

"It's him!" Radiant's voice was low and reverent.

Aegis's heart sank in her chest. Oh, no.

Holloway righted himself and glared up at the floating man. "I was hoping you'd be the one to fall into my trap!"

The floating man shrugged lazily. "Maybe send an engraved invitation next time, Holloway. I'm a busy guy."

"I have no doubt," Holloway retorted. "Why don't you come down here and fight me?"

"Because it's not time for that yet," the man replied, his voice light. "Right now, I'm just the distraction."

Holloway froze. "The what?"

Then Aegis heard it: a loud roar, like a charging bull. A massive vehicle burst from the trees, looking like a runaway tank. It bounced once, then careened across the field. Just as it was about to slam into Holloway, a side door opened and a figure dove from the vehicle, the ground lifting to catch whoever it was. The vehicle slammed into Holloway, knocking the monstrosity back. Holloway cried out as he toppled over.

The driver sprang to his feet. He was wearing dark armor, his legs gray and black mottled camouflage. His shirt was black, with thick black gloves. A hood covered his face, and black fabric covered his face. The man clawed his hands, then forced them together. The ground underneath Holloway bubbled and then surged over him, encasing him in dirt. The man twisted his fingers, and the dirt shimmered, turning into solid metal.

"Can you believe it?" Radiant whispered. "It's them. It's them! It's Failstate and Gauntlet!"

Aegis nodded numbly. She should have expected this.

The man in black turned to face them. "Are you two okay?"

"Doing better now that you're here," Radiant called, her voice bright.

Aegis wished she could be as enthusiastic.

Gauntlet gently alighted next to Failstate and clapped him on the back. "Good work, partner."

Failstate stumbled forward, then turned to face the other hero. "You didn't just throw your motorcycle at him, did you?"

"Maybe."

Failstate groaned.

"What?" Gauntlet smirked at his partner. "You hit him with your car."

"My car can take that kind of abuse," Failstate retorted. "That's the fifth motorcycle this year. The VOC isn't going to keep buying you new ones."

"You said distract him."

"I didn't mean to toss a motorcycle at him."

"Hey, it worked." Gauntlet laughed.

Aegis gaped at them. How could they be so casual, bantering like that? Entombed in dirt just behind them was a colossal horror, and...

The ground beneath her trembled and bucked. Failstate and Gauntlet whirled just in time to see Holloway burst from his metal prison. His tentacles thrashed, tossing chunks of metal the size of boulders in all directions. Radiant ignited one of her lightblades and sliced through one of them. Another slammed into Aegis, knocking her off her feet but otherwise not hurting her. Gauntlet batted another one away, and Failstate held out his hands, the clod dissolving into nothingness.

"You dare?" Holloway thundered. "You dare try to entrap me?"

"Well, yeah!" Gauntlet retorted. "Kind of our job."

"Don't antagonize the body horror!" Failstate grunted.

Once again, Aegis was struck by how calm the other two heroes were. She supposed that made sense. These two held official government vigilante licenses. They had saved the world dozens of times in almost as many years. They had faced down monsters before, many of them worse than this. Even still, how could they be so calm? Aegis felt her heart slamming against her ribs, hard enough that she was sure she would pass out. How were they going to win this fight? Sure, there were four heroes fighting just one villain, but Holloway was so huge, so overpowered. No matter what they threw at him, the metallic octopus just shrugged it off and kept lashing at them with tentacles. Aegis could feel the cracks radiating through her armor plating. The few times she peeked at Radiant, she realized that the other girl wasn't able to even scratch Holloway's metal exterior. As for the two licensed heroes...

Suddenly, Gauntlet burst from the ground, rocketing straight for Holloway's face. He smashed his fist right between Holloway's eyes. The blow caved in the villain's face, ripples flowing through his body like waves. Had they finally struck an actual blow against the monstrous creature? But the waves slowed and then froze in place before flowing backward, his features reverting to normal.

"Are you kidding me?" Gauntlet shouted.

As if to answer, a tentacle slapped him out of the air. He crashed into the ground shoulder-first, plowing a deep rut into the ground. He clambered back to his feet and somehow, his costume was completely free of dust and dirt. He still patted off his arms and legs, then turned to Failstate.

"I think it's time for you to bring out the big guns," Gauntlet said. "I think it's our only option."

Failstate grumbled something under his breath, but nodded. "Okay." He turned to Aegis and Radiant. "Brace yourselves."

For what? But he never explained. Instead, he clenched his fists, drawing his arms to his chest. At first, Aegis couldn't figure out what he was doing. But then she felt a shift in the atmosphere, as if the air was suddenly filled with static. While she couldn't be certain, it almost appeared as if a halo of energy flickered around Failstate's body. Even Holloway seemed to notice. He stopped attacking Gauntlet, Radiant, and her, and rushed for Failstate.

Before the villain could reach him, Failstate cried out and threw his arms open. A wave of pins and needles swept over Aegis, quickly passing through her body. A few moments later, Holloway shrieked, his voice pitching up higher and higher until it turned into a badly distorted wail. Failstate groaned and collapsed to his knees, nearly pitching over onto his face.

His metallic body started to bubble and roil, and then his massive form collapsed to the ground. The silvery metal turned liquid, flowing across the ground as it melted. Within seconds, the prone human form of Dr. Holloway appeared, lying in a puddle of silvery goo that sloughed off his arms and legs. Aegis risked approaching him, but she quickly realized he wasn't a threat anymore. He gasped like a fish out of water, his chest heaving, and he struggled to even rise. His body appeared even more gaunt and withered than before, and he wore only a pair of white pants that clung to his stick-thin legs.

"Wh-what did you...do to...me?" His voice was raspy and weak.

"My partner can disrupt electronics. He's basically a living EMP weapon." Gauntlet chuckled. "Maybe not the best choice to turn yourself into some freaky cyborg octopus when he's around, huh?"

Before Holloway could respond, Gauntlet picked the man up by his chin, then smacked him with his other hand. Holloway pinwheeled through the air and collapsed in a heap ten feet away. Gauntlet glanced at his hand, apparently noticing the silvery goo that clung to his fingers. He shook out his fingers, disgust twisting his features.

Relief swept through Aegis, but then something that Gauntlet had just said popped into her mind. Failstate could disrupt electronics? Like maybe...

Radiant gasped and whirled on her. "The woman!"

Aegis nodded, her eyes wide. They both turned and hurried toward the cylinder.

"What woman?" Gauntlet called after them.

Aegis spun around. "We found a woman in Nexora. She's the Prime Component for PanOptic? She's on some sort of life support, but if Failstate fried the system—"

Suddenly Gauntlet was right in front of her, grabbing her by her shoulders, staring at her with a fierce, almost frightening intensity. "Where is she?" He shook her. "Where?"

"In the cylinder," Radiant said.

Gauntlet looked to where Radiant was pointing, and he sprinted over to it. "Failstate! Failstate, get up!"

With a groan, Failstate got to his feet. He turned and jogged after his partner. Gauntlet skidded to a halt at the cylinder and drove his hands into the metal, punching through the seam between the doors and then peeling them open. He ripped them off the cylinder and tossed them over his shoulder. They spun through the air and then slammed into the ground twenty feet away.

"Is it...is it her?" Failstate called.

Gauntlet whirled on him. "I think it is!" Desperation flowed through his voice.

Aegis ran up to the cylinder. Thankfully, the woman looked no worse for wear, given the wild ride she'd been on that night. But much to Aegis's horror, she stirred. Her eyes fluttered open. She gasped, trying to say something, but couldn't because of the tubes that ran in and out of her mouth. But then her gaze locked onto Gauntlet, and her eyes went wide. She tried to say something.

Gauntlet reached into the cylinder and took her hand, his motions surprisingly gentle. "It's all right, Liz. I'm here. You're going to be okay."

Aegis looked at him and then did a double take. Were those...were those tears in his eyes?

"I'm going to get her to a hospital," Gauntlet announced. Then he bent down and lifted the entire cylinder onto his back. He flexed his legs and leaped into the air, then flew off.

Aegis watched him go, stunned. What was that about? She turned around to see if Radiant had any idea...

Instead, she found herself face to face with him. With Failstate.

With the man who killed her father.

*Now's your chance, Marisol! Prove to me you're a loyal daughter! Kill him for me!*

Even though his face was hidden as always, she could feel the weight of his gaze on her. She tried to stand straighter, taller. She was even tempted to thicken her armor, if only to make herself look more imposing. But she didn't. There was no point. She knew he wasn't a threat, not to her.

"Marisol," he whispered, his voice drifting off as he stared at her. "You, uh...you handled yourself well tonight. Your family..." His shoulders shifted, almost as if he was wincing. "You should be proud."

Ice sliced through her. She knew what he had almost said. Her father's voice continued to rage, but she did her best to blot it out. She wasn't about to seek vengeance on Failstate. For one thing, she knew her father hadn't given Failstate a choice.

For another, she knew how much the hero regretted what had happened.

"Thank you." She forced the words past her clenched teeth.

It looked like Failstate wanted to say more, but he didn't. He nodded once, sharply, then cleared his throat. "And you too, Radiant. Keep up the good work."

Radiant gasped, her eyes wide and shining. Then Aegis heard them: the distant wail of sirens. They grew louder, and soon she saw the flashing red and blue lights drawing nearer. Failstate turned back to Dr. Holloway, who was finally struggling to his feet. The hero made a motion with his hands, and the ground underneath him rose, encasing him up to his neck. Then Failstate started toward the nearest road, presumably to greet the police.

Aegis watched him go, her heart twisting. She should have felt happy, even satisfied. She had done what she had started out to do. Project PanOptic was done. Dr. Holloway had been exposed. And she had even earned praise from one of the top superheroes in the world. So why did she feel so empty?

Radiant touched her arm, and she turned to face the other girl. Aegis's shoulder slumped as she remembered what she had confessed in the lab. Now Radiant knew the truth about who her father was and what he had done.

The other girl studied her face and then nodded. "Thank you. Not just for tonight, but for telling me the truth. I know that must have been hard for you."

Aegis blinked, trying to hide her surprise. Radiant's words sounded genuine enough, but she wasn't sure how she should react.

"And hey, you know my name now," Radiant continued. "Look me up. Maybe we could go out on patrol sometime." She offered Aegis a hesitant smile. "I mean, we kind of make a good team, right?"

Once again, Aegis didn't know how to respond, but she managed a quick nod. Radiant studied her face for a moment, and then headed in the same direction Failstate had walked, calling after him to let her catch up.

Aegis watched her walk away. She turned back to study the Nexora campus once more. When she first came here earlier in the evening, she had worried that she was making a mistake. What kind of difference could she make against such a powerful corporation? Now, though...

A smile tugged at her lips. She wasn't her father, and she didn't have to run from his shadow anymore. Maybe that was what being a hero really meant—standing in the light, even when it hurt.

# Notes on "Project Panoptic"

THIS ONE... YEAH, IT might take a little explanation about what is going on.

My debut novel, *Failstate*, was published in 2012. I wrote it as a standalone story, but I left the ending open enough that sequels could be written. Shortly after it was acquired, the publisher asked if I had any ideas for sequels.

I didn't at the time, but I sat down and came up with three more book ideas that would expand Failstate's storyworld. Most significantly, I wanted to give Failstate an arch-nemesis. I needed to come up with someone who would be a good counterbalance to Failstate and his powers. The result was a super-hero-turned-villain. His superhero name was "the Dallas Dillo," and his power was creating organic armor underneath his skin. Because of an encounter he had with Failstate, the Dillo became a supervillain (with no name at the time) and became the Joker to Failstate's Batman. He would pop up throughout the three books I had planned, making life difficult for Failstate.

My publisher was not impressed with my ideas and asked me to go back to the drawing board. My idea for the Dillo got scrapped (and probably a good thing too; I think I may have stolen his name from DC Comics's *Captain Carrot and His Amazing Zoo Crew*. Yes, that's a real comic series). Instead, I wrote two more books: *Failstate: Legends* and *Failstate: Nemesis*.

Even though the Dillo wasn't in those books, he lingered in my imagination. Although I don't remember consciously doing this, I think I may have recycled my ideas for the Dillo into the Baron from "Upstart." And while the Dallas Dillo isn't mentioned in the Failstate trilogy, he is a part of my head canon. And since I'm Failstate's creator, that means he's officially part of the story.

Over the years, I've toyed with the idea of returning to Failstate's storyworld. I have a loose outline for a book about Etzal'el, a powerful hero who shows up in *Legends* and *Nemesis*. A few years back, I had a glimmer of an idea set ten years after *Nemesis*. But nothing ever really came together.

Until the fall of 2025, that is. As I was getting ready to teach freshman English again, I had this wild idea: what if I used *Failstate* as part of my class? What if my students had to discuss characterization and story arcs and theme with the author of the book they're reading? I got permission to go ahead, and that's what I did.

It was an interesting experience. Not all the kids enjoyed it, but a few really got into the story. One student read all three books within a week. Another drew fan art of the main character. But one girl became heavily invested in Failstate's love life.

See, in *Failstate*, there's a love triangle that develops between Rob, the main character, Ben, his brother, and Elizabeth, a girl at their school. Who is Elizabeth going to choose? My student had a very strong opinion about what should happen. Extremely strong. So much so that when she found out that I went in the opposite direction, she spent a week glaring at me every chance she got.

Naturally, being the mature person that I am, I decided to twist the knife a little. The result is this story.

I decided I had to bring closure to that love triangle. And what better way to do it than to officially bring the Dillo into the story?

Will this be the last time we see Aegis and Radiant? I have no idea. If you had asked me a year ago if I'd ever write another Failstate story, I probably would have said no. Yet here we are. So I guess the right answer is "Never say never."

John is a PK, a pastor's kid. He grew up in Columbia Heights, a suburb of Minneapolis, with his parents and younger sister and brother. They were the terror of their local library because, every few weeks, they would come and check out crates full of books, increasing the workload of the poor librarians. In high school, though, John worked at the same library, so it balanced out.

After high school, John attended Concordia University in St. Paul, Minnesota, where he majored in theatre. Upon his graduation in 1996, he moved on to Concordia Seminary in St. Louis, Missouri. He graduated with his Masters of Divinity in 2000. He served as a Lutheran minister in Blue Earth, Minnesota, and South Saint Paul, Minnesota. He currently work as an English teacher in the Kansas City area, where he lives with his wife and kids.

John is a lifelong writer. He started with badly drawn comic books in the fifth grade. When he realized that he was a lousy artist, he moved on to badly written novels in middle school. He's tried his hand at screenplays (don't ask), stage plays (a little better), fanfic, teen mysteries, and religious fiction. But his first love has always been speculative fiction.

His debut novel, *Failstate*, was published by Marcher Lord Press in April of 2012, and was a finalist for the Christy Awards in 2013. He has gone on to publish four more novels with Marcher Lord Press/Enclave Publishing, two of which, *Numb* and *Failstate: Nemesis*, were finalists for the Christy Awards in 2014 and 2015. *Drawn in Ash* won the Realm Award for Science Fiction in 2023 and was a semi-finalist for the Carol Awards that same year. *Drawn by Light* won the Carol Award for Speculative Fiction in 2025.

John looks forward to telling even more strange tales that point people back to God and His incredible grace.

## ALSO BY...

**The Failstate Series**

Failstate
Gauntlet Goes to Prom (ebook exclusive)
Failstate: Legends
Kynetic: On Target (ebook exclusive)
Failstate: Nemesis

**The Ministrix Duology**

Numb
The Hive

**The Legacy of Ink Trilogy**

Drawn in Ash
The Storm's Eye (ebook exclusive)
Drawn through Blood
Drawn by Light

Cage and the Outpost of Monolith (short story)
Cage and the Warden's Secret (short story)

## Anthologies

Into the Bewilderness
Just Dumb Enough (Contributor)
The Memory Eater (Contributor)
Spirited: 13 Haunting Tales (Contributor)